Shad

Catherine Lucy Czerkaw̶̶̶̶̶̶̶̶̶̶̶̶ ̶̶̶̶Leeds in 1950 and brought up in Ayrshire. She has had poetry and a historical monograph published and SHADOW OF THE STONE is her first novel for teenagers. It has previously been produced in the form of a television series.

CATHERINE CZERKAWSKA

Shadow of the Stone

Richard Drew Publishing
Glasgow

First published 1989
by Richard Drew Publishing Ltd
6 Clairmont Gardens, Glasgow G3 7LW
Scotland

The publisher acknowledges the financial assistance of the
Scottish Arts Council in the publication of this book.

British Library Cataloguing in Publication Data

Czerkawska, Catherine
  Shadow of the stone.
  I. Title
  823′.914[F]

  ISBN 0-86267-259-7

Set in Chinchilla by Swains (Glasgow) Ltd
Printed and bound in Great Britain by
Cox & Wyman Ltd, Reading

For Alan, with love

Acknowledgment

Many thanks are due to Leonard White without whose patience, enthusiasm and invaluable suggestions the original television serial which preceded this novel would never have been made.

She erupted from the gates of the school and ran down the road like one possessed, a battered bag clutched across her chest and long dark hair flying out behind her. She did not see, or perhaps deliberately ignored the boy who had been waiting for her. He made as if to follow her but then, shy of being seen to run after a girl, changed his mind, slowed and stopped. 'Liz,' he shouted after her. 'Oh hang on Lizzie,' but Elizabeth ran on, blind and deaf to him.

Tom was a good looking, gentle faced boy of seventeen. His grimy overalls proclaimed him to be working, something which many of his friends might have envied him. He did not feel enviable. He had left school the previous summer to help with his father's yacht charter business but he did not enjoy his work. Kate, pretty and self confident, approached him. She liked Tom but his attachment to Liz irritated her. She was impatient with his continual submissiveness. 'Leave her alone Tom,' she said to him, taking a small mirror out of her bag and examining her make-up closely. She was very fair with bright blue eyeshadow framing blue eyes. Her hair stood up like a golden halo around her head. 'Why don't you go and wash some of that muck off your face?' Mr King had hissed at her in assembly that morning, but she had ignored him as usual. His bark was much worse than his bite. All the kids liked him, all except Lizzie of course. She hated him but everyone knew why that was. 'Why can't you leave Liz alone?' Kate said to Tom. 'She's crackers. You know she is. She doesn't give a damn about you. Forget about her.' Tom glared at her then relaxed into a slouch. 'She'd rather talk to her lizard,' continued Kate and burst out laughing. 'Lizzie and her lizard.' Tom had that kind of face, she thought, a victim's face. He had always been soft. Too nice for his own good. You could get away with murder with him. Kate liked her men to be tough and domineering. She enjoyed being told what to do.

'What would you know about it anyway?' Tom kicked at the wall, scuffing his shoes.

'You're just like a little kid,' she told him.

'I don't care.' He liked Kate well enough but not when she was scathing about Liz. As always, he felt torn between loyalty to

Elizabeth and the need for sympathy in his predicament.

'She's crackers I tell you,' Kate reiterated. Then, relenting, she put her mirror away and took Tom's arm. 'Ah come on,' she said. 'Let's not argue. Last day of term.'

'Not for us working men.'

'All the more reason for you to treat me. You can buy me a Coke if you like.'

She steered him off in the direction of the town centre. 'I'm meeting Jim when he finishes work. You can keep me company till then.' Tom meekly let himself be led away. If Liz didn't want him, he might as well go with someone who did.

Elizabeth ran on through the streets of the little Scottish seaside town. It had rained earlier that day, as it had rained almost every day that summer but she splashed heedlessly through puddles, with an increasing sense of elation. Last day of term and the holidays stretched before her. And now that she was sixteen there was another thought, dangerous and tantalising. She didn't have to go back to school. Not ever. Her mother and her grandmother wanted her to stay on. If she was honest with herself she had to admit that she probably would stay on for another two years. But she didn't have to. She felt happiness welling up inside her. After the rain, the town smelled of summer: the sweet-sour scent of privet hedges and the perfume of cut grass. She had left all her companions behind. None of them could keep up with her. Not one of them.She shook her hair back from her face, eyes sparkling, a small, dark, odd looking girl with a single-minded,curiously elated expression that caused passers-by to turn in amusement or perplexity and stare after her. She paused only when she came to a narrow gap between two old greystone buildings on the main street of the town. Then she stopped so suddenly that a party of elderly day-trippers in polyester macs bumped into her. They apologised indignantly but she ignored them. There, leading up the steep hill that rose high above the shops and harbour was a flight of worn stone steps. She hesitated for a second and then, taking a deep breath like a swimmer about to dive into a pool, she plunged up them.

Away out in the Clyde Estuary, a solitary yacht glided into view, approaching the town and its nearby marina. There was only one passenger aboard, both skipper and crew. He was a wiry athletic man in his mid thirties, wearing tattered cut-off jeans and a white tee shirt with a faded motif of an old sailing ship on the front. He looked tired and rather scruffy, his dark curly hair streaked with the blonde of constant exposure to sunlight, but when he stared towards the town that clambered up and over the hills above him his blue eyes lit up. He looked all around, across to Dunoon and the sea lochs beyond, the highland hills dappled by constantly changing cloud shadows, drawing the eye ever on and on. So this is it, he thought. This is it at last. His spirits rose and a smile of pure joy illuminated his rather thin face.

The yacht was a Freedom, with two masts and an unusual rig. Her name was painted on the transom: *Marie Lamont* in fancy black and gold lettering, which seemed a curiously Scottish choice for a boat that was flying the Stars and Stripes, alongside a courtesy Ensign. The man stood up and began to furl in the sails. He had almost reached his destination.

Liz was climbing the stone stairs, not slowing in her headlong charge until, breathlessly, she reached the top of the flight, where a panorama of the sea below and the hills beyond suddenly opened out. Tenement houses rose still higher behind her. In front, and to one side, the cliff fell steeply away to rickety old buildings, the backs of high street shops, beneath, but here on this little eyrie in the middle of the hillside, stood an old grey monolith hemmed in by iron railings and with a bench beside it. People had carved their names into the wood of the bench and the more determined had chiselled initials into the monument itself. Mutely, the stone had rejected their pathetic attempts at immortality for who now remembered the AL who had once loved MK?

As Liz stared at the old stone, a great longing came into her face. She walked around the railings as far as she could go, for on one side they ended in solid rock and on another in a steep drop to the town below. Then she stretched out her hand in between them, to touch the stone with her fingertips, glancing quickly over her shoulder to make sure that no intruders were listening. This ritual was intensely private. 'Granny Kempock, Granny Kempock help me,' she whispered. It was not enough. She knew instinctively that she must be closer. Her whole body must be in contact with the solid rock. She put down her bag and squeezed through, where somebody before her had bent the metal apart, grazing her shins in the process but almost uncaring and certainly unaware of the pain.

3

Aboard the *Marie Lamont,* the stranger turned on his engine for the final part of his journey. Liz could not see the yacht from where she stood. Besides, she was totally absorbed in the stone. She hugged it awkwardly, spreading her fingers out across the surface. It was warm to her touch as if it had absorbed some of the day's sporadic sunshine. Then she whispered, 'Granny Kempock! Granny Kempock!' She might have been speaking to a real woman of flesh and blood and not an old stone with a heart of hard implacable stone to match. A watcher would have shivered at the uncanny intensity of the plea but the stairs were deserted.

The sailor, intent on his approach, glanced upwards towards the stone for an instant. Once, when the town was little more than a row of cottages with a kirk beyond, it would have been clearly visible from the sea, a marker for the fishermen, but gradually the town had encroached on and around it. Elizabeth spoke aloud, hands, arms, breast and cheek still in contact with the stone. 'I wish, I wish,' she muttered. Her eyes were closed. Then a shudder ran through her, she released her hold and climbed quickly back through the railings. She went up the remaining steps and to a higher vantage point from which she could see the whole bay with its little ripples and eddies and changes of colour spread out before her. There was only one boat to be seen and it was heading straight for the marina. Liz clutched her bag against her and screwed up her eyes again. 'Please Granny Kempock,' she said aloud. 'Please let it be this summer. Please!'

A hand fell gently on her shoulder from behind. 'Elizabeth!' She started violently then relaxed. It was her grandmother, Rose, smiling at her. 'You were miles away. Penny for your thoughts.'

'Do you really want to know?' asked Liz. She could tell her grandmother anything at all. Her love for the elderly woman burned bright and fierce, inside her. Sometimes in the early hours of the morning she would lie awake worrying about what she would do if Rose were to fall ill and die.Such things were inevitable after all. Occasionally glancing at her grandmother, she would be suddenly aware of wrinkles, of the fatigue behind the eyes, and then she would be horribly afraid. She took Rose's arm confidingly.'If you want to know, I was asking the stone for something.' Rose raised her eyebrows in mild surprise. 'Granny Kempock? What on earth for?'

'Oh no.' Liz moved away, looking out to sea again. 'You mustn't tell when you make a wish.That way it might never come

4

true.' She turned to face Rose. 'Do you think I'm daft?' Rose hugged her affectionately. 'No,' she said. 'Of course not. What's wrong with wishing?'

'People used to ask her for things so why not me?'

'Aye,' said Rose, 'but look what happened to them.'

'That had nothing to do with Granny Kempock.' Liz stared out to sea, lost in her own private world. 'That was just silly people. People being afraid.'

Rose shrugged. 'I'm not sure I should approve of all this superstition.'

'Well,' said Liz slyly. 'You were the one that told me, weren't you? You started me off.'

'I know I did.' Rose followed Liz's gaze out to sea. 'Beautiful boat,' she said.

'Do you see the rig?' asked Liz, staring at the yacht. 'Unstayed masts. It's a Freedom.'

'How on earth do you know that?'

'Oh you'd be surprised what I know!' The rain was past. The afternoon sun was turning hills and waves one gold. 'Do you think she'll help you, old Granny Kempock?' asked the older woman, after a pause. 'Do you think she'll grant this wish, mm?'

When Liz spoke it was with enormous certainty. 'Oh yes. I'm sure of it.' She watched the Freedom turning into the mouth of the marina. 'I wished hard enough this time,' she said. 'It felt right. You'll see.'

Rose frowned a little, faintly worried by the intensity with which her grand-daughter spoke.

'Come on,' she said lightly. 'Time we were at home. You must be hungry.'

The two set off from the stone, walking up the hill to where big Victorian houses marched along in ostentatious rows. This had once been the prosperous part of town. Now it was merely suburban, most of the houses divided into flats.

'Where's mum?'

Rose hestitated, before replying.

'Gone to the supermarket I think.'

'Oh yes?' There was a question in Liz's voice which Rose chose not to answer. But the girl stopped suddenly. She had seen a car approaching, an XK Jaguar, cult car, renovated, clean as a new pin and polished every Saturday with tender loving care.

'Oh God,' said Liz. 'Him!' She left Rose's side abruptly, ran through the gate of a large sandstone house and up the outside

5

stair to the upper flat, fumbling for her key as she went. Rose waved at the occupants of the car. Alice was a fair haired woman of about forty with something of Rose about the eyes and Liz about the mouth. The man behind the wheel was Danny King: large, thickset, though not unattractive. A little older than his companion, he could never quite throw off his air of being a teacher. Occasionally he would aggravate adult friends by barking at them to, 'Sit down' or 'Hurry up for goodness sake!'

Rose smiled at them both and raised her hand again in greeting as the car drew up outside the house. Then she followed her grand-daughter up the stairs in a more leisurely fashion.

The back of the car was full of brown paper grocery bags bristling with cans and packages and loaves of wholemeal bread for the freezer. Liz's mother Alice was determinedly 'into' health foods. Danny made as if to get out and begin unloading but Alice detained him. He relaxed in his seat and turned to face her, wondering, as he had so many times before, how such a pleasant normal woman as Alice could produce such an odd unmanageable girl as Elizabeth. At sixteen, one surely couldn't put it down to adolescence any longer. It wasn't a phase. It was just Liz. He blamed the father, the absent divorced father, now living in England with a new family and never really interested in his first, indeed his only daughter. And he blamed Rose too for encouraging the girl and for indulging her, though he could not help liking Alice's mother. The similarities between Liz and her grandmother were marked, even more marked than those between mother and daughter. But Rose had all the wisdom of her years. She was invariably steady and good humoured, if a little eccentric.

Danny had done his best to make Liz like him. Over the past year while he had been going out with Alice he had tried in all possible ways to endear himself to the girl, but there was always such a huge gap between his good intentions and the outcome of his efforts. He would plan over and over again what to do or say and then when he was confronted by Liz's surly or sarcastic face, everything would go wrong. He would strike out verbally, and she would respond in kind. Alice would be angry with her and angry with him and there they would be, back to square one again. It didn't help of course, that he had been teaching her at school for the past two years. Nor did it help that he taught maths which Liz hated. Perhaps the thing that angered him most of all was that she was a clever girl and could have done well if she had put her mind to it. He would have sympathised more had she been a complete dunce at his subject. He could have laughed about it then and tried to help her and perhaps she would even have been grateful. But her mind was quite simply elsewhere. Danny sighed aloud. Alice laid a hand on his arm and looked up at him pleadingly like a dog after a bone.

'So?' He jiggled the ignition key nervously. He put on his strong, manly, capable voice. He didn't feel very capable where Liz was concerned but that didn't matter. Appearances mattered.

'We must tell her,' said Alice.

'Of course we must.'

'The trouble is, I keep waiting for the right moment but it never comes. I thought if you spoke to her. . . .'

Danny said nothing. He had a sinking feeling that was curiously akin to fear. Danny King: afraid of a teenage girl? Never! He coughed to cover his confusion. It was unlike him to feel so helpless.

'She's just going through a bad patch,' continued Alice. This was what she always said when trying to justify her daughter's rudeness or bad behaviour. Yet Liz was seldom rude to anyone else; only him. 'Look Ally,' he said, determined to speak out. 'She's been going through a bad patch as you call it, ever since I started going out with you. I mean we pussyfoot around each other at the best of times don't we?

'She's not going to be pleased, whoever has a word with her. But she'll just have to get used to the idea. That's all there is to it.'

'She hasn't had a good year at school.'

'I did my best,' said Danny indignantly leaping to his own defence. Alice frowned. Why was everyone so prickly these days and she could have been so happy too? She was happy. She loved Danny. Danny loved her. He wanted to take care of her. It was years since anybody had wanted to take care of her.

'I know, I know,' she said reassuringly, patting his arm. Danny sighed again. It wasn't Alice's fault after all. 'Sometimes,' he said, with a rueful smile, 'I think that if I came to school wearing yellow wellies and a peaked cap she might like me better.'

'Oh that,' Alice shrugged. 'It's all dreams you know, that sailing business.' She paused. 'I ask you — Liz — sailing! Mother just encourages it. But maybe mother could have a word with her. Smooth things out beforehand I mean.'

'Maybe that would be best.' Anything for a quiet life. Danny got out and began to unpack the bags of groceries. He saw Liz watching him from the top step, frowning down at him. As usual the scowl stung him, disproportionately. 'Come on,' he said, aware even as he spoke that he was using the typical tones of a teacher. 'Come on Dopey, what are you standing about there for? Give us a hand!' He turned abruptly away before she could reply and continued to unpack the bags.

The Finlays, mother, daughter and grandmother, lived in a large flat with inconveniently high ceilings and vast windows which took up the whole top floor of a big stone built house. The building had once been the home of a rich Glasgow merchant, his large family and servants, but his day was long gone. The flat was all light and splendid sea views but impossible to heat and difficult to furnish, since the rooms dwarfed all modern furniture. Just to curtain the windows had cost a king's ransom. Fortunately Rose had brought some good pieces of furniture with her from her old home. Old sideboards and wardrobes that had looked monstrous crammed into Rose's small house suddenly assumed gracious and pleasing proportions when placed in these larger rooms. They belonged.

Alice, who had always lived on a tight budget, haunted the local auction rooms until she found other pieces at reasonable prices. There were three bedrooms, a big kitchen and a bathroom which was also of Victorian proportions. There was an old enamel bath, possessing an extraordinary and daunting plunger arrangement instead of a plug and a high ostentatious lavatory with a warm wooden seat. There was an enormous light, bright sitting room, part of which they used as a dining area. The room had a high moulded cornice with grapes and vine leaves and a centre rosette. Alice lived in fear of dry rot ever since she had enquired about the cost of replacing the cornice but so far they had been lucky.

The whole flat was pleasantly cluttered and invariably dusty. There were books everywhere, since Rose and Liz were inveterate readers and great collectors of second hand reading matter from jumble sales and Oxfam shops. Neither could ever bear to throw anything away that might just possibly be of interest in the future so that strange mouldy volumes on foreign travel, written in the last century and illustrated with water colour prints showing 'Zulu Warrior' or 'The Bridge of Sighs' rubbed shoulders with fifty year old books on home improvement and Latin grammars, annotated by forgotten scholars in faded ink. Alice, on the other hand, collected china: plates, jugs, teapots and splendidly useless ornaments. There were home made rugs on the floor, from Alice's rug making phase, a few years previously, and pretty embroidered cushions from when she had attended an evening class last winter. Alice sampled various crafts for a couple of years at a time. She had a natural talent but soon she would grow bored and drop each in favour of the next interest. So far, and much to Liz's disgust, she had shown no signs of wanting to drop Danny.

Liz, at the sound of Danny's voice, had simply turned around and disappeared indoors again. 'Why should I help him?' she muttered.

'Liz,' shouted Danny, stung to anger.

'Oh leave her alone.' Alice frowned at him. 'Come on. We'll take them up together. We don't need her. Leave her be.'

In her bedroom, Liz squatted down in front of a glass cage like a little aquarium. It was full of stones and heated to a comfortable temperature. Inside, basking on a rock, was a miniature dragon. The lizard stared at her impassively and flicked its little tongue in and out. 'You know, don't you?' she said aloud. 'You know!'

The room was a shrine to sailing and the sea. The walls were covered in pictures of yachts, pictures of the great races and other mementoes. One wall was a shrine to Claire Francis and Naomi James, with photographs and news clippings. There was an old embroidered picture of a sailing ship and a shelf of sailing books, old and new. There were glass floats and shells and a big white fender that she had picked up on the beach one day. There were anonymous bits of wood and rope that she had found on the seashore and imagined as belonging to some sailing vessel of the past. There was a book on knots and some practice specimens laid beside it. In pride of place was a piece of scrimshaw: an intricate whalebone carving depicting walruses and polar bears, which her grandmother had bought for her last Christmas. The room was an enthusiast's paradise, but Liz stayed where she was, squatting morosely in front of the lizard's cage until she heard her mother calling her.

'Come on Lizzie. Your dinner's ready. Hurry up!'

Then, she slouched into the sitting room. Danny, Alice and Rose were already seated around the table. There was a big bowl of salad, a plate of cold meat and a mountain of chips in a serving dish. They often had chips when Danny came to dinner as Alice yielded to his less conscientious eating habits. Liz liked chips too but she always refused them in Danny's presence. And he was present more and more often now.

'I don't want anything,' she said, pulling a face at the meal. 'I don't like cold lamb. It's horrible.' She went over to the window and looked out across the bay, down towards the tantalising expanse of sea. For as long as she could remember she had loved the sea and for as long as she could remember her mother had refused to take that love seriously.

'Come on Lizzie,' Alice had told her, even as a small child. 'You can't spend all day just staring at the water. Come on home now!' She remembered first becoming aware of the sea. The size of it stunned and exalted her. It seemed to go on forever, and she found that obscurely comforting as well as amazing.

Her father had been just as bad. 'Come on Lizzie Dripping,' — his pet name for her — 'time to go home.' Sometimes she thought that she might explode with the longing for the sea that raged and fermented inside her. Why wouldn't they understand? She thought that their lack of comprehension must be deliberate for surely her desire to sail could not be made any plainer. At the age of ten she had built a raft and set sail in it from the beach but her knots had been inadequate. The wooden planks had come adrift and floated away and Liz had had to swim for the shore. Her clothes had been ruined. It was March, the water was icy and she had caught a cold. As usual she had brought nothing but trouble on herself. Now that she was older, her mother simply humoured her. Danny laughed at her. Only Rose sympathised.

'Come and eat please Liz,' said Rose and Liz suddenly guilty, came and sat beside her and took a little meat and salad but no chips.

'What are you planning to do with your holiday Liz?' asked Danny pleasantly. This surely was a safe subject.

'I don't know.'

Liz looked from her grandmother to her mother and made a supreme effort to be friendly. 'It'll soon go won't it?'

'I used to hate having to go back to school after the holidays,' said Rose. 'There was always so much more to do at home. Don't you find that Liz?'

Liz nodded enthusiastically.

'It was one of the chief pleasures of growing up,' Rose continued. 'I mean not having to go back to school on Monday mornings and at the end of the holidays. I don't know how

10

you can bear it, Danny, even if you are on the other side of the desk.'

'Oh I like it well enough.' It was true. The job excited him. He still liked his subject enough to wish to communicate it to others.

Rose shrugged. 'Of course. It's your job.'

'Anyway, I don't have to go back now,' said Liz. 'Not now I'm sixteen. Not if I don't want to.' Rose intercepted the quick worried glance that passed between Danny and Alice and shook her head ever so slightly. There was silence. No-one rose to the bait. Liz looked around with a flushed angry face, daring them to argue, then turned her attention back to her meal.

'You're a bad influence mother,' said Alice lightly. 'I used to enjoy school and I don't mind going back now.'

'Ah but that's different. You're in the office, not the classroom. Classrooms always have that dreadful smell of wood and chalk dust, or they did in my day.'

'And sweaty feet and disinfectant,' said Liz. 'They still do. It's horrible. I hate it.'

'There you are then,' Rose patted her hand. 'We're two of a kind, aren't we Lizzie?'

'So we are. I wonder where you come in, mum?'

'Now,' said Rose. 'Don't you be cheeky.'

Danny laughed too but he could not keep the edge of censure from his voice when he said, 'I don't think Liz deserves a holiday this year.'

Liz was piling lettuce on to her plate, more than she could ever eat. 'Why not?' she asked, aggressively, not looking at him.

He was committed now. 'Well you haven't exactly killed yourself with overwork at school have you?'

Liz was immediately on the defensive. 'I tried.' She put some lettuce back in the bowl.

'Oh Lizzie!' Alice took the salad servers from her and laid them down. 'That's enough now.'

'I'm sure you did try,' said Rose, pacifically.

'Everything got on top of me this year.' Liz spoke directly to Alice, ignoring Danny. I'm sick of fighting with him, she thought. Why does he always do this to me?

'I know Lizzie. I do understand.' Alice was trying to be sympathetic.

'Mind all at sea eh?' broke in Danny. Alice kicked his shin under the table.

'Ouch,' he said.

11

Liz frowned.'Yes. It was all at sea but you wouldn't under-stand, would you?'

'Try me.'

She shrugged hopelessly, got up and left the room.

'You always do that,' said Alice unhappily.

'I only meant to make her laugh.'

Rose refused to join in. She got up and went to find Liz.

'She thinks we criticise her all the time,' said Alice. 'Maybe we do.'

'If she can't take a little harmless criticism. . . .' Danny stopped. He hadn't wanted to get involved in any arguments, but they seemed to happen in this house in spite of himself.

'You must try harder,' Alice was pleading with him. 'You must make her like you.'

'How, for God's sake?'

'I don't know. But you've got to try.'

Rose found Liz in the kitchen, chopping up a piece of raw meat into fly sized bites, for her lizard.

'Danny means well,' she told the girl. 'You are a bit touchy you know, Liz.'

Liz carried on chopping, viciously. 'Why does he always have to stick his oar in?'

'He probably worries about you.'

'Well he shouldn't.He's only my teacher. Not my father. Yet.'

She gathered up the meat into a dish and left the kitchen abruptly. Rose felt suddenly very tired. This isn't my problem, she thought resentfully. I've been through all this the first time round with Alice. I'm too old for it now. I'm tired of it. She sat down on the kitchen stool and poured herself a cup of coffee from the jug that stood ready under the filter machine. I wouldn't mind being on my own for a little while, she thought as she sipped. The coffee was too weak as usual. She suspected that Alice infiltrated the decaffeinated stuff into the tin. 'Why shouldn't I have a good strong cup of coffee if I want to at my age,' she said aloud to relieve her feelings. 'I don't care if it is bad for my heart.' I need my freedom too, she thought.

In her room Liz fed the miniature dragon and then threw herself restlessly on the bed. It was still light, the sun declining slowly, casting long sharp shadows. She could hear seagulls squabbling out on the water. She got up and walked about the room, trying

12

to dissipate her anger. It was pointless and unfair to vent it on Rose who was her only ally. She arrived at the window and looked down into the bay. A little way off she could just make out the very tips of the tallest masts in the marina.

She began to change out of her navy uniform into jeans, tee-shirt and canvas shoes. She brushed her hair and tied it out of the way, then crept out of her room. They would be talking about her now, analysing her problems. Danny would be pretending to be sympathetic and worried. Rose would be genuinely so, and her mother, as usual, would be caught in the middle, not knowing what to make of it all. She tiptoed across the hall, wary of creaking boards, then out of the door, closing it gently behind her. There was a sudden burst of laughter from the sitting room: Danny's loud infectious bellow. Perhaps they were laughing at her, but she didn't care. At least they hadn't heard her go. She was down the outside stair and off in the direction of the marina before they had even noticed her absence.

The marina was just outside the town where a concrete break-water protected an already sheltered bay. A cluster of new buildings had sprung up around the main marina office housing a chandlery and restaurants, as well as the offices of charter companies and yacht sales agents. Beneath the marina office were shower and toilet blocks and it was from one of these that the yachtsman appeared with a damp towel slung over his shoulder and whistling cheerfully. He looked altogether fresher and neater, his hair clinging in damp tendrils to forehead and neck. He paused to survey the marina, then walked down towards the pontoons.

The marina was quiet at this hour. The chandlery had closed for the day and the restaurant was only just gearing itself up to meet the evening onslaught. Liz came marching bravely in at the gates. A large part of her free time was spent at the marina and she knew her way around. To her left was the little boatyard owned by Tom's father. Drawn up on the hard there was an old wooden fishing boat which Bill Henderson was renovating with — according to Tom — a great deal of blood, sweat and tears, not to mention recriminations for having undertaken the project in the first place. 'He's making my life a misery over it,' Tom told her. 'I wish he'd just shut up and get on with it.'

Bill Henderson was hoping to be able to charter the boat the following season, though looking at it, it seemed an unlikely possibility. Liz glanced around for Mr Henderson but he was nowhere to be seen. She passed the little cabin that was his charter office but that too was closed up and empty. He often worked late, but today he must have gone home early for once. She was relieved. She disliked Tom's father almost as much as she disliked Danny. He had several boats: a couple of high ugly motor cruisers like floating garages and two small yachts that he ran as 'bareboat' or unskippered charters. People simply hired them and took them away for a week or two. Frequently they ran them aground on sandbanks, less frequently on islands, and had to be towed off. Henderson always checked their qualifications but it made no difference. Even the most highly qualified skipper seemed to be capable of horrendous indifference to the fate of a hired boat. Sometimes they ran out of gas and sometimes they blocked up the sea toilets and sometimes they did unspeakable things to the engines. Almost every week, during the season, Bill Henderson would be called out to rescue one or other of his charterers. This perhaps went some way towards explaining his hostility towards Liz and what he saw as her romantic notions of sailing. It always astonished and pained Liz that Tom took almost no interest in his father's business beyond what was essential so as not to incur parental wrath. Tom preferred to paddle around the harbour in a little Mirror dinghy without sails, and fish for codling by the hour. He wouldn't take Liz aboard the Mirror however, and Mr Henderson was equally deaf to all entreaties that he might take her out on one of the yachts when it wasn't booked.

'This is business Lizzie,' he told her. She hated being called Lizzie except by her immediate family. 'I'm not an instructor and I need all the time I can get to work on these boats, when they're not being chartered. You should see what people do to them. You try unblocking a sea toilet or two once a week and then see how you feel about the glamour of sailing. Huh!' He was a good natured man but quick tempered. It was hard to believe that Tom, always the easygoing, gentle daydreamer, could really be his son. Liz wanted to tell him that she wouldn't mind unblocking a dozen sea toilets if only he would please teach her to sail, but she couldn't bring herself to say it. She could see that he considered her a nuisance.

A little hesitantly, she sidled into the marina office and up to the desk. She knew the two officials slightly and she smiled at them ingratiatingly. 'Excuse me, but did a Freedom come in here

14

today?'

'Why would you want to know?' asked the younger of the two.
Liz blushed. 'I'd just like to see it please.'

'Oh aye?' The older man smiled at her. He was tubby and grey
haired. He had always been pleasant to her, so far. 'Thinking of
buying it are you?' Liz smiled too. The young man looked over
the top of his gold rimmed spectacles at her. She couldn't tell if he
was joking or not.

'Only boat owners allowed on the pontoons,' he said sternly.

'But I always go down there!' Almost every weekend, summer
and winter alike, she took a walk along the pontoons to see
which boats had come and which had gone and which — as many
did — stayed there for years on end and never moved. How
criminal, Liz thought, to have a boat and not to use it.

One elderly couple used their little motor cruiser as a holiday
home. They would arrive on Friday night or Saturday morning
with boxes of groceries and a portable TV set and they would
spend their weekends harmlessly pottering about on board, the
husband touching up his varnish, the wife knitting on deck in the
sunshine, reading the *Daily Express* or Mills and Boon romances
and sometimes baking cakes and biscuits in her little gas oven.
Mr and Mrs Mackenzie had grown used to Liz and she to them.
They would smile and wave at her and several times she had run
errands for them to local shops for milk or teabags. In return she
had been invited aboard to drink tea and eat home-made cake.
The cabin was bright with pot plants and crocheted doilies, pictures of kittens and Spanish dancers. Liz made allowances for
the Mackenzies. She liked them well enough. But tonight she
was intent on finding out about the new boat, wanting to know
who was aboard it, wanting a closer look at it.

'I always go down to the pontoons,' repeated Liz plaintively to
the marina official.

'Then you shouldn't, should you?' replied the young man
severely.

'But I only go to look. Has anybody complained about me?'

'Not yet,' he admitted.

'Besides, I have friends with a boat.' This was her trump card.
'The Mackenzies. Aboard *Spanish Lady*.' The name always
seemed singularly inappropriate for the tubby and less than
flamboyant cruiser.

The older man smiled at this. He knew all about the Mackenzies. 'Oh aye?' he said again. Poor kid, he thought.

15

'There's always a first time,' said the young man, somewhat pompously. 'For complaints I mean.'

'Please,' Liz looked at his companion.

'Pontoon A. Berth number 25,' said the older man briskly. 'But don't get in the way. He'll be wanting his rest.'

'What do you mean?'

'He's come from the States.'

'To here?'

'To here.' He smiled at her surprise. 'So don't go bothering the man will you?'

'No. No I won't. Thank-you.' She turned to go. 'What's his name?'

'Steve. And remember,' put in the young man, 'the first complaint will be the last.'

'I will.' She hurried out.

'Crazy girl,' he said. 'Boat mad.'

'Harmless.'

'I hope so.' The young man shrugged.

'Anyway, it's not my problem I'm glad to say.'

Liz hurried down the pontoon treasuring her gem of information. It would do for an introduction. The sleek thirty-six foot boat, looking surprisingly clean and neat for all the distance it had sailed, was neatly tied up alongside the pontoon. A few casual observers were strolling past to look at it. Liz slowed down feeling suddenly nervous, feeling the familiar twisting sensation in the pit of her stomach. She almost turned and walked away again. Tomorrow would do. She was too shy. She would just admire the boat from a distance and go home. But then she saw the name painted on the transom: *Marie Lamont*. Her heart gave a great thump of excitement and she crept a little closer, touching the yacht with a tentative hand. A tall suntanned man was sitting in the cockpit drinking from an unfamiliar can. Beer, she guessed. He had a book open on his lap and was idly flicking through it, half looking at the pages but now and again glancing diffidently up at his admirers on the pontoon. She willed him to look in her direction and it seemed that the suggestion was a powerful one because he did indeed turn towards her and smile casually. The grin seemed somehow to light up his face. It reassured her. 'Hello,' she said. 'Are you the person that's come all the way from America?'

'Across the pond? Yes. No great shakes . . . everybody's doing it.'

'Not alone.'

The man shrugged and drank some more beer. Liz summoned all her reserves of courage. 'I saw you come in earlier this afternoon,' she said. 'It's a Freedom, isn't it?'

'That's right.' He was casual but not unfriendly.

'She's lovely.' Liz patted the boat. 'I've read about this kind of boat. This kind of rig I mean. But I've never seen one.'

'Glad you like her.' He closed his book. 'Not everyone does.'

'Why not?'

'Too easy some say.'

'Oh?' She wondered what to say to cover her ignorance. There was a pause. Perhaps a knowing silence was best. The man stood up. Please invite me aboard she thought. Oh God why wouldn't he? Please. He moved to go below. 'Excuse me,' he said, very politely. He was tall, when he stood up with the muscular physique of a sportsman. Liz said quickly, 'Could I come aboard? Have a look?' Steve's eyes flickered over her, noticing her properly. She's very young, he thought. No more than a kid. But he saw the desperation in her eyes, He saw that this was something more than the casual allure of a suntanned sailor for a young girl on the threshold of womanhood. He knew that he was attractive but he had long ago ceased to take conscious advantage of his looks. It was too easy, too unrewarding. He had had a steady relationship with a woman back home; one of the teachers at his East Coast sailing school. She had been a divorcee with a young child. They had a lot in common but he had not felt ready for the responsibility of marriage with a ready-made family and so they had split up. Whenever his friends and relatives spoke to him about 'settling down' he could feel some wild familiar impulse rise in him to confound them all again by leaving everything behind and sailing off into the blue. That had been the pattern of his life so far and he had no reason to expect it to change now. He had no intention of ever settling down. Sometimes in his darker moments he thought that this perhaps indicated some failure in himself — this inability to sustain a relationship. But since he was happy to be a wanderer, why should he try to adapt himself to suit other people's expectations of what was normal?

Who will show me the far horizon, without obstructions to the view, he thought. He had read somewhere that in the Dark Ages, Celtic monks had set sail in coracles, wishing 'for the love of God

to be anywhere.' He could well understand that primitive longing to sail away. His ancestry was Scottish and he often felt that
he had been born at the wrong time; that he ought to have
been one of those ancient adventurers when all the maps were
guesswork and all foreign lands enchanted.

But sometimes in the nights he was lonely for the touch and
warmth of humankind, of womankind. And no casual encounter
ever quite satisfied the cold empty feeling that just occasionally
descended on him.

He looked at the girl closely. 'Could I come aboard?' she
pleaded again.

'Just quickly then,' he said, with some reluctance. 'I've got to
go ashore soon. Find a payphone.'

She swung herself on to the boat. She might be any age
between fourteen and twenty he thought. It was so hard to tell
these days. 'I can show you where the phone is,' she said, eagerly.

Not as much as twenty, anyway.

'Thanks,' he said.

'So you really have come from the States?'

'Yes. Really.'

'In this?'

'Sure.'

She was deeply impressed. 'It's wonderful. Wonderful.'

'Would you like a Coke?' Steve asked her, his natural polite-
ness reasserting itself. Besides, he was touched by her enthusiasm. 'One left I think.' He scrabbled about in the bottom of a
locker and came up with a can of Coke and another can of beer.

'Thanks,' she said. He didn't offer her a glass. Liz sat blissfully
in the cockpit and drank Coke from a can. It seemed a very American thing to do. People, wandering down to look at the boat,
would see her and think that she belonged. She could pretend
just for a moment that she was part of this wonderful world of
yachts and yachting and casual invitations aboard.

'I'll need to get some fresh food in,' said Steve. 'I'm sick of tins.
I think I'll eat out tonight though. Know any good places?'

'Not really.' Liz wished she was knowledgeable about such
things. Her family seldom ate out in the town. 'There's a Chinese
and an Indian place. We go there sometimes. Oh and there's the
Marina Restaurant of course. Up there. That's supposed to be
good.' She looked around the boat as she spoke.

'It's so strange,' she said, eventually. 'How do you work her?'

'Easy once you get the hang of it,' he told her. 'You don't sail?'

There was a fraction of a moment's pause before Liz answered. 'Oh yes. Often.'

'Does your family have a boat here then?'

'No. No.' Be careful Liz, she thought. You're in deep water here. 'Just with friends — you know,' she added.

'Mhm?' said Steve non-committally. He opened his second can of beer. Liz stared at him in fascination until he became uncomfortably aware of the intensity of her gaze. 'Is there something wrong with my face?' he asked. She must be very young after all, he thought. No older girl would be quite so obvious in her admiration.

Liz was surprised. 'What?'

'I've only just got rid of the beard.' He rubbed his chin that was a little paler than the rest of his face. 'Coming up the Clyde. But I don't have two heads do I? Unless I sprouted one in mid-ocean. Funny things happen at sea.'

Liz laughed, embarrassed. 'Oh no,' she said. 'You're OK. You're fine. What's your name? I'm Liz.'

'Steve,' he told her.

'And why is she called *Marie Lamont*? Your boat?'

'She was one of my ancestors,' he said, lightly. It was as though everything had fallen suddenly into place for her. Everything would happen just as she had wished. She could hardly believe it. Thank you Granny Kempock, she thought. Aloud, she said, 'Marie Lamont lived here. Did you know that? Is that why you came?'

'One of the reasons.'

'I'd love to sail like you. You don't know how much I want to sail.' She sipped at the Coke, making it last, making the moment last, giving herself time. Why, when you were blissfully happy, did the time just slip away?

'What's to stop you?' asked Steve.

'Oh all sorts of things.' She put down her empty can and made a half hearted attempt to leave. 'You'll be needing your sleep. I'd better go. They told me not to bother you.'

'What I need is a real meal.'

'How do you manage?' she asked suddenly curious. 'About sleeping? Out there?'

'Self steering system.' He indicated the rather cumbersome mechanism. She nodded as though she were familiar with it though she had never noticed such a thing before. But then few people in the marina would have need of such a piece of equipment, when a long voyage was a trip through the Kyles of Bute and perhaps as far as Tarbert.

'That can't keep watch, can it?' she said. 'Weren't you afraid of being run down by something in the night? They can't stop for miles, can they? Those supertankers?'

'Five miles they say,' Steve spoke laconically. 'But that's the kind of risk you have to take. I made it, didn't I?'

'Will you be staying here long?' Her fingers down beside the seat were crossed. Steve didn't notice. Granny Kempock loomed up in her mind. She wished hard. Steve shrugged. 'I'm not sure. I don't like to plan too far ahead. A few days maybe. A few weeks even.' Her fingers relaxed. Thank you Granny Kempock.

'Have you been here before?' she asked him.

'No, but my great grandparents came from this area. Robert and Isabella they were called. Quaint eh? I've always had the notion to come over and see the place for myself. Where do you live?'

'Up in the town. Up the hill there.'

'Won't your mother be wondering where you are?'

Liz was sensitive to hints. She stood up. 'I'm sorry. Look, I'd better go. I must be bothering you.' Her tone was almost hostile. Steve relented. 'Oh you're not bothering me.'

Liz immediately and cunningly took advantage of this softening. 'Would you take me for a sail sometime?' she asked. Steve, looking at her hopeful young face found it impossible to refuse. 'Maybe,' he replied tentatively. 'How old are you? Fourteen? Fifteen?'

'Sixteen!' She spoke with such indignation that he believed her.

'Anyway, you'll have to check with your mother. I can't take you unless she agrees.'

'I will. I promise. And you'll show me how to sail her?'

'Oh you shouldn't find it too difficult. Not if you've had some sailing experience.' When Liz did not reply he only smiled at her. Let it be, he thought. He would find out soon enough if she had been lying to him. 'OK?' he said, pointedly, standing up.

Liz clambered down on to the pontoon. 'I'll see you tomorrow then.'

'Tomorrow?' He was taken aback but he had committed himself. He always kept his word. 'I suppose so. Tomorrow then. But not too early mind. I need a good rest.'

Liz almost danced home. She went up the little flight of stone steps and past Granny Kempock. Everything was meant. Everything was right. Marie Lamont. The boat was called *Marie Lamont*. Liz knew all about Marie, for three hundred years ago she had wished on the Kempock Stone too, just as Liz herself had wished today. She had wished for a boat and now here it was.

That night she found it very hard to go to sleep. The lizard too was restless in his glass cage. She had left her curtains undrawn. For a while she could hear the muted rumble of late traffic passing through the town below and the calls and whistles of Friday night revellers walking home from the seafront bars and discos, but presently all fell silent and there was nothing but a faint swishing that might have been the wind or the sea. She couldn't tell.

Moonlight shone in at the window falling full and silver on her face, gleaming on her dark hair, creating eerie shadows in the corners of her room and making her dressing table mirror shine with a faint incandescence. She had read for a little while, as usual, before switching off the light, but now she lay in that uncomfortable state somewhere between sleeping and waking when full consciousness and sound sleep are equally unattainable. Her book lay open on the bed. In the moonlight, the illustration was fully visible: an old engraving of the Granny Kempock Stone, by night, with weird figures posturing and capering around it in a grotesque travesty of a dance.

Liz tossed and turned and muttered on the bed. And then she spoke. Her voice was odd, slightly hollow and her accent much broader than her everyday tones. There was a curiously old fashioned lilt to it, though the sentiments were very much her own.

'Why should a lassie not go to sea?' she said. 'What's wrang wi' a lassie on a boat? Tell me. Why should I bide at hame washing pots and pans and clowts for the rest of my life? That's all the water I ever see.' Her eyes were closed but she was not quite dreaming. It was more as if a film were being played out against the screen of her eyelids. But as in a dream she was powerless to control the images that came and went there.

She saw a girl standing, half turned away from her, in a small room, up in the eaves of a cottage: a net loft perhaps. She was a pretty girl but angry, black hair straggling around her flushed face, feet planted squarely on the wooden boards. 'Why should a lassie not go to sea?' she said again. The girl swung around full face and with a shock of recognition Liz saw herself. It was not a mirror image for this girl lived and breathed and moved quite independently of the dreamer. The scene was at once strange and yet vaguely familiar. She should have been afraid but she felt only an intense involvement, an identification with the girl's thoughts and feelings.

She moved restlessly on the bed and as she did so, the curtains moved also in a sudden breeze. The moonlight shimmered and shivered over the white bedspread and over the picture so that the little figures appeared to move too, caught in their endless dance around the stone.

Aboard the *Marie Lamont* Steve was having a similarly restless night, tossing and turning, while the Freedom rocked gently at her pontoon. He groaned in his sleep and threw off the quilt, though the night was chilly.

Liz still spoke aloud. She might have been arguing with somebody though the other party to the discussion was invisible.

'I'm as good as any fisher lad,' she said indignantly. 'It'll dae ye nae skaith tae tak me wi' ye. It'll not hinder ye frae killing the fish tae hae me aboard. Can ye not tak yer Marie wi' ye? Oh why not?' Her voice became anguished. 'Why not?' The lizard sat still and startled in the moonlight.

'Why will ye not let me gang wi' ye?' said Liz so vehemently that one would have expected her to wake herself up. 'I'm as good as any fisher lad,' she continued. 'It'll dae ye nae skaith!' Her voice had risen from a low murmur to a stridency that was audible outside her room. It woke Alice who came rushing in, in her nightdress but stopped dead when she saw by the light from the hallway, the girl's closed eyes. 'Tak me wi' you,' pleaded Liz. 'Tak me wi' you. Don't listen to them.' Alice put her hand on her daughter's shoulder and shook her gently.

'Liz. Lizzie!' she said. 'You're dreaming.'

Aboard his boat Steve was suddenly jerked awake, as if he too had been shaken into consciousness. His body and quilt were bathed in sweat. He climbed unsteadily out of his bunk and looked outside at the now muted lights of the town. The dream had immediately slipped away from him but still he shivered, his mind full of some terrible foreboding of violence, some great concentration of hatred. What had it been? It was fading too fast for his mind to grasp. Only the tattered remains of words and

22

phrases were left running disjointedly through his head. 'Take me with you?' A strange emblematic dream. A stone and a ship and a bonny red gown. That was it. He repeated the phrase over to himself but could make nothing of it. A stone and a ship and a bonny red gown. And then the dream was quite gone, leaving only the fear behind it.

He went back down to his cabin, switched on the lights and drank a glass of mineral water. No point in trying to sleep just yet. He picked up the book which he had been looking through the day before. It was an Edwardian guide book for this part of Scotland that had lain in his New England family home for years, and the same book that Liz had been reading before she fell asleep. Steve flicked through it again and it fell open at a picture of the Granny Kempock stone. There's my 'stone' anyway, he thought idly, as he began to read.

In her room Liz sat bolt upright, eyes staring, breath indrawn, then relaxed. 'Mum!' she said with some relief. Alice sat down on the bed and switched on the lamp. 'What on earth were you dreaming about?' she asked. 'It sounded like a nightmare. That was why I woke you.'

'I don't know,' Liz frowned. 'It's gone. It wasn't very nice.'

'No more cheese sandwiches before bed,' Alice laughed. 'And who's Marie, for goodness sake?'

She looked at her daughter. The girl's eyes were closed again.

'I am,' she said in a low distinct voice. Alice felt her scalp tingle. She reached out and touched Elizabeth's arm.

'Don't Lizzie,' she said uneasily. 'Don't do that. It gives me the creeps.' Liz opened her eyes with a start.

'What?' she said.

'Nothing.' Alice fussed around her, plumping up pillows, straightening the covers. 'Just the dream I expect. Go back to sleep now.'

Liz sat up clasping her knees.

'What happened?' she asked.

'You were just talking in your sleep.'

'Was I?' Liz spoke slowly. 'I remember now. I thought I — was someone else.'

Alice picked up the book. 'You were reading much too late you know. I got up to go to the loo at about midnight and your light was still on.'

'What time is it now?' Liz yawned.

'About three.'

'Did I wake gran?'

'I don't think so.'

'That's gran's book.' Liz pointed to the little guide book she had been reading. 'All about the Kempock Stone.' She sank back on the pillows, her eyes already closing. 'All about poor Marie Lamont. All about. . . .' Her voice drifted into an incomprehensible murmur, then silence. Alice closed the book and put it on the bedside table. She crept out, switching off the light and grimacing at the lizard as she passed by. He had frightened her at first. Now they maintained casually friendly relations. She had expected him to be slimy. Instead he was cool and dry and quite pleasant to the touch. Not at all what he seemed.

She went back to her own bed. Liz was an imaginative girl. The book had made an impression on her. That was all. There was surely nothing to worry about. It had been just a dream she thought. Just a dream. Still, she found it very difficult to go back to sleep again that night.

MARIE: 1662

It was five years since. I was just a lass of eleven. Kettie Scott — she was our neighbour — she learned me to take kye's milk. She was dairy maid over at Blackhall. We would go out very early in the misty mornings before the sun was up and take with us a piece of hairy twine and draw it over the mouth of a mug saying 'In God's name, God send us milk. God send it and meikle of it.' And then the mug would be full of milk. No — I don't rightly know how it was done or if she would maybe milk the cow herself, but I know we got much of our neighbour's milk that way and Kettie made butter and cheese at Blackhall and for her own family too. I haven't tried it since. Well, I tried it once on my own but no milk came and I got feart and left the mug, twine and all in our neighbour's byre.

When I was fourteen, I told my father I wanted to go to sea. The lasses, they go up to Kempock and they ask the auld stane there for a husband. They carry a basket of white sand seven times widdershins around the stone and make a wish. It is not witchcraft, no, they are all good God fearing lassies. But me — I asked the stane for a boat. 'Oh Granny Kempock send to me a fine wee boat to cross the sea.' That was a rhyme Kettie tell't me to say, so I did.

My cousin Thomas, he was seventeen. He had his own boat: a

wee coble. He went to the fishing in it. Once he took me out in it between Inverkip and Gourock and I was sick. I told Kettie and she gave me a phial of something. It was very pleasant with a taste of ginger and herbs and there was a charm to repeat three times and then I was well. I lo'ed the fishing. I aye knew where the best herring were. Thomas got the best catches and all when he had me in the boat with him. He said I was his luck. We were hand-fasted though my mither said I was ower young to marry and should maybe wait a year or two. So you see Granny Kempock had sent me a husband and a boat as well. Or so I thought.

2

There had been more showers in the night but they had passed, and now brilliant sunshine gave the normally sombre West of Scotland seafront a cheerful continental air. But perhaps it was just that Liz was looking at the place through new and more enthusiastic eyes. She could almost feel at home here this morning. She paused at the top of the stairs beside the Granny Kempock stone. She mustn't disturb Steve yet. 'Not too early,' he had said. She mustn't push it too far; mustn't spoil things by being childish. Nevertheless she found it impossible to stay in the house. She would go to the café first and tell the others all about it.

In the *Two-Oh-Two* coffee bar which faced the main street of the town and backed on to the seashore Kate and Tom were sitting looking out to sea.

'Did she say she was coming?' asked Kate.

Tom shook his head. 'But we always come here first don't we? She knows. She'll come.'

It was a tradition with their crowd: the *Two-Oh-Two* on Saturday mornings, early in summer and a good deal later in winter so that they could decide what to do with the rest of the day. The choice was severely limited: there was very little to do in this small seaside town if you were short of cash and most of them were perennially short of cash. Tom worked for his father but Mr Henderson was not over generous. 'You get your keep don't you?' he told Tom. 'Big lad like you. Got to work for your keep.' What Tom really wanted was to work on the fishing boats but Mr Henderson looked askance at this. 'There's a perfectly good job here lad,' he said. 'And the business'll be yours after I'm gone. It's too risky at the fishing. The work's hard, the hours are long and it's too bloody dangerous altogether. Why make trouble for yourself?' Tom could seldom summon the willpower to argue with him. 'You have to be brought up to the fishing lad,' Henderson always finished triumphantly. 'You don't know your own mind. You stick with your old dad and forget all this nonsense about fishing.'

Kate, still at school, was hoping for a Saturday job in a hairdressing salon, although the position would not be vacant for

26

another month. She wanted to take an apprenticeship in the same salon. She always contrived to dress in the height of fashion on a small amount of money. She was handy with a sewing machine and created some of her more outrageous garments herself. She spent half an hour or more every morning on her makeup and pretended to be impatient with Liz's lack of interest in her appearance, her customary jeans and teeshirt and her occasional and limited use of lipstick and eyeshadow. In fact she had grown used to her vision of Liz as a plain, quirky girl who presented her with no competition at all, a convenient sort of friend and a continual boost to her own self image. So she was surprised and not entirely pleased when she looked up from her Coke to see Liz strolling in looking unusually smart in clean pressed jeans and newly whitened deck shoes, a pink fluffy sweater and anorak.

'I wonder what stories she'll be telling us today?' Kate whispered to Tom. He had visibly brightened when Liz came into the café. He ignored Kate's remark and went over to put coins in the jukebox. Liz ordered a coffee at the counter and walked across to join Tom. She was bursting to tell her friends about Steve. Nothing so exciting had ever happened to any of them.

'I tried phoning you last night,' said Tom reproachfully. His choice of music was always heavily romantic. She suspected that it was all aimed at herself but she steadfastly refused to be moved by it. How could she be? She had known Tom for almost the whole of her life. They had beaten each other over the head with toys at nursery school and had gone on to attend the same primary school, albeit a class apart. They had both been well behaved little children paying attention with a solemn intensity that amused their teachers. Because their parents had known each other they had played together and attended each other's parties right through primary school but when they moved up to the town's large comprehensive and although Tom was a year older and a year ahead Liz seemed suddenly to have outstripped him. Her father had left home and Liz had changed too. She grew impatient with Tom's caution and his gentleness. She was quicker and more intelligent than he, but the teachers liked her less because she was less law abiding, less popular, and this hurt Tom. He always wanted everyone to like Lizzie and defended her staunchly against all attacks.

When Tom was fifteen and Liz fourteen Kate told her, 'He fancies you you know.' Liz could hardly believe it. 'Don't be daft,' she said. 'Not Tom. He knows me too well.' But gradually it became apparent to her that it might be so. Since he was ten Tom had messed about the harbour in a little dinghy without sails.

'If he fancies me so much why won't he take me out on his boat?' said Liz angrily to Kate. Tom went fishing every weekend but he always excluded Liz from these trips no matter how she pestered him.

'Lassies are no good on boats,' he told her which was something he had once heard his father say. By the time he was fifteen he had some inklings of regret that he had taken this stance but he stuck to it for another six months before finally asking Liz if she would like to accompany him. It was too late. She refused indignantly, partly to annoy him and partly because she had decided that she hated killing things.

'I can't bear fishing,' she told him. 'It makes the boat stink. It makes you stink.' She wanted to sail. Tom had tried sailing with his father but he hadn't enjoyed it much. Besides he had a sneaking suspicion that Liz might be better at it than he. She usually was better at most things.

'Why not give it a try?' he asked. 'You never know. You might enjoy it.'

'Not fishing. Sailing.'

'I can't sail. I don't know how.'

'You won't you mean!' she rounded on him. 'And besides, lassies are no good on boats. Isn't that right? I wouldn't come with you now if you paid me, Tom Henderson.' So there matters stood. Now that he wanted her, she seemed to be avoiding him. She had carried on avoiding him for the last two years. The more she did so, the more he wanted her, thought about her, dreamed about her.

'Did you phone?' asked Liz. 'Nobody told me.' She remembered now that Alice had mentioned it.

'You were out.'

'That's right.' Liz was noncommittal. Tantalisingly she pretended not to notice his curiosity. Kate came over to join them. Liz relented or perhaps it was just that she couldn't bear to keep the news to herself any longer.

'I was down at the marina,' she said casually. 'I met this guy down there.'

'Oh aye?' Tom sounded half disbelieving, half worried.

'What's all this then?' demanded Kate. 'What guy?'

'He just sailed over from America.'

Kate groaned and leaned on Tom's shoulder. 'Haven't they

all,' she said. 'Boring. Boring.'

Liz turned away and sat down at a table with her coffee. She scraped her teaspoon over the surface, scooping up the foam and put it in her mouth. 'OK,' she said. 'If you don't want to hear. . .'

'But I do,' said Tom desperately.

'He's got a Freedom.'

'What's that when it's at home?' asked Kate.

'It's a special kind of a boat. You know, don't you?' Liz looked at Tom. He nodded.

'Sort of. I don't know much about it though. I'd have to ask my dad.'

'Never mind about the boat. What's this guy like?' asked Kate impatiently. 'Is he good looking?'

'He's nice.'

'Dishy?'

'I suppose so,' Liz shrugged. He was, but she wasn't going to admit as much to Kate. She thought about him, seeing in her mind's eye the tanned face and strong brown hands. Yes, he was really quite good looking. She drank her coffee.

'How old?'

'Not all that old. Mid thirties I think.'

Tom finished his Coke. 'You want to watch it,' he told her.

'Older men. Yummy,' added Kate. She got up, 'Come on you two.'

'My records are still playing,' said Tom plaintively. Two elderly ladies, drinking morning coffee, looked at them disapprovingly. They wore crimplene dresses and hand knitted cardigans and carried large straw bags with coloured flowers on the front. They were obviously on holiday. They didn't appreciate Tom's choice of music.

'I like older men,' said Kate as they wandered outside.

'I like his boat,' said Liz. 'I love his boat.'

High fluffy clouds were bowling across the sky. There might be rain later but not yet. The weather would hold for her first sail.

'So what are we going to do then?' asked Kate. Tom said nothing. He looked miserably across at Liz. A good looking boy of about eighteen wearing baggy jeans and a French cotton knit sweater had come up behind them. He put his hands over Kate's eyes. She squealed and held on to his arms. 'Is there anything exciting to do?' she asked. 'Take me to London Jimmy.'

'Don't be daft,' said Jim, nuzzling into her neck, behind her ear.

'We could take the ferry to Dunoon.'

'Oh brilliant. Really exciting.' Jim groaned. He worked in a garage and was the only one of the four with any money but after he had paid his way at home and bought the clothes that were his passion, there was very little left.

'It's better than hanging around here anyway,' said Kate. Jim turned to Tom and Liz. 'Where do you want to go?' Jim's arrival had effectively made them into two couples. Liz was sorry for Tom but she shrugged off the feeling. She couldn't help that look in his eyes could she? 'I'm going down to the marina,' she said as casually as she could. Tom fell right into the trap she had placed for him. 'Oh not again,' he groaned. 'Nothing to do but look at boats. I'd sooner go to Dunoon.'

'That's just as well then isn't it,' said Liz sharply. 'Because I'm going for a sail and you can't come.'

'Who with?'

'This guy I met last night.'

'You're kidding.' Kate was all agog.

'No I'm not. He's asked me out for a sail.'

'My God,' Kate laughed. 'Lizzie's done it. She's finally got somebody to take her out on a boat.' But there was an undertone of jealousy in her voice.

'He teaches sailing back home in America,' said Liz by way of explanation. 'He's taking me out for a lesson.'

'I'll bet,' said Jim. 'You, sailing? You must be joking.'

'She's lying as usual.' Kate put her arm in his proprietorially.

Liz shrugged. It didn't matter whether they believed her or not. 'You'll see,' she said.

'Does your mum know?' asked Tom jealously.

'Why?' Liz pounced on him angrily, black hair flying. 'Were you going to tell tales?'

He stepped back in alarm. Sometimes she almost frightened him. He never could face her anger. 'Well — you know. Going out on a boat with a stranger,' he finished lamely.

'He's all right,' said Liz. 'I do know him. I've waited all my life for this. For this boat I mean. All my life.'

'I never knew you wanted to sail,' said Jim interested in spite of himself. He had only been going out with Kate for a few months and was a comparative newcomer to their group.

'That's all she ever talks about,' said Kate spitefully, holding him close, 'boring, boring, boring.'

Liz always marvelled at how the presence of a boy could completely alter Kate's atttitude to her girl friends. It was as though she suddenly saw all of them as competitors. Liz had never noticed this failing in her other friends but Kate, like Tom, had a jealous streak. Liz couldn't be bothered arguing with her. There was no point. She turned away, looking at her watch, then set off towards the quay. Tom followed her and presently the other two strolled after them.

The town had once been a prosperous little port with pleasure ferries leaving for Dunoon and the islands and sailing to and from Glasgow but that had been during the heyday of the Clyde Coast when foreign holidays were beyond the reach of most people. Now there were signs of neglect over a large part of the harbour and further along the shore were empty and overgrown swimming pools. But perhaps things were already changing again. There was a new ferry terminal from which there were regular sailings to and from Dunoon; a great deal of new building was going on in the town and after years of decay it seemed as if another corner had been turned in the history of the place.

Liz walked swiftly past the terminal, ignoring the ferry which was preparing to leave. Tom caught up with her in a last desperate attempt to persuade her to change her mind.

'Go on,' he said. 'Come to Dunoon.'

'I don't want to. I'm going to the marina. I've been to Dunoon hundreds of times.'

Tom hesitated. 'You go,' she said vehemently. 'I've got better things to do.' She set off swiftly, leaving him standing, looking after her.

'Are you coming?' Kate asked him.

He turned away. 'No,' he said not looking at the pair of them, not wanting to meet the sympathy in their eyes, afraid of finding scorn there too. 'No. I'll not bother.'

'Sure?'

'I don't want to play gooseberry. On you go. You'll miss it.'

'OK. Suit yourself.' Kate and Jim boarded the ferry. Tom was left on his own to watch their departure, as the boat pulled away to Dunoon.

'Damn Lizzie,' he thought. A couple of years ago she might have relented and then they would have had a great day; a good laugh together. Now she didn't want to know. He had tried going out with other girls to make her jealous but it didn't work. She just let him get on with it and wished him well. He couldn't bear it: the fact that she didn't seem to care at all. Often he had fantasies about her, about kissing her, touching her, holding her close, even making love to her though he had made love to nobody yet. When his friends said they had done it he boasted too but he wondered who they all thought they were fooling and how many of them, like himself, were just afraid of losing face. He wanted her companionship as much as any physical relationship. More in fact. He would analyse the things she said to him, hoping to pluck from her words some crumb of the old easy affection that had once existed between them but now it seldom came.

'I'm that sorry for him,' said Kate aboard the ferry. She leaned her head on Jim's shoulder. 'He should've come. He's daft about Liz.' She waved to Tom, a dwindling morose figure on the quayside. Then she moved to sit in comfort cuddled together with Jim. It was a typical morning aboard the Dunoon ferry. Somewhere a senior citizen's outing was having a sing-song.

'I don't think she's natural,' said Kate. 'She cares more about her pet lizard. I mean to say. A lizard.'

'It's not your problem is it?' Jim pulled her closer and kissed her. 'Anyway I don't mind if it's just the two of us. Do you?'

'No,' said Kate. 'I don't mind at all.' They kissed again. A small child, licking a lollipop, came up very close to them with solemn curious eyes.

'I'd go away if I were you,' said Jim to the child. It was dressed in pink and blue tee shirt and shorts and could have been a boy or a girl. It had spiky hair and its mouth was red and sticky from the lollipop. It gazed at them with unwavering blue eyes, ignored Jim's advice and continued to suck its lollipop. "We'll meet again,' sang the senior citizens and swayed in time to their own music.

The sound drifted back to Tom as he watched the ferry move out of sight; then he too slowly moved away. He found that he was walking in the direction of the marina.

The marina was much busier than it had been the previous evening. The car park was full and there was the usual bustle of weekend sailors, preparing to leave or simply staying aboard to get on with the hundred and one little jobs they had been putting off since the previous autumn. The Mackenzies were there as usual. Mrs Mackenzie was arranging a vase of sweet williams at her little sink. She waved to Liz. 'Tea?' she asked.

'Not this morning thanks,' Liz called to her. 'I'm going out on a boat!'

'Are you? Good for you!'

Steve was standing on the pontoon hosing down his yacht. He looked up to see Liz approaching him and an expression of mild dismay crossed his features before he could compose himself to meet her. He had been half hoping that she would have decided not to come. After all, he wanted a break from teaching. Still, there was something so intense and unusual about her that he couldn't bear to disappoint her. Liz caught the regretful expression immediately and her heart sank. He's changed his mind, she thought. 'Am I too early Steve?' she asked quietly, stopping at the end of the pontoon. Steve found it impossible to rebuff her. It all seemed to mean so much to her. He wondered why. He didn't for one moment believe that she was familiar with boats but surely she could have found somebody to take her sailing before now.

'No. You're not too early.' He smiled at her. 'You might as well stay now you're here.' He wound up the hose. 'Did you ask your mother?'

'Yes of course. She said it's OK. Isn't it a lovely day?'

Steve nodded.

'Did you get a good meal last night?' she asked. She was looking at him as if he were some kind of God. A few years ago he might have been tempted to take advantage of that look. Now it only afforded him a certain wry amusement. I must be getting old, he thought. But she's such a child.

'Well I thought it was a good meal,' he said aloud, 'but I didn't sleep too well after it.'

'Neither did I. I was too excited about today I suppose.'

He climbed aboard. 'Come on then,' he said. 'Single up.'

Liz stood looking tentatively at the yacht. 'Sorry,' she asked, frozen to the spot. 'Sorry. What did you say?' Single up? What could he mean?

Steve pointed to the appropriate ropes. 'Take off the springs there. The ones that are holding the boat off. Do you see?'

Liz did so rather hesitantly and much relieved that he had helped her out.

Steve started the engine. 'Now,' he told her. 'Let go the head and stern ropes and hop on.' She untied the ropes clumsily, her fingers scratching at the thick fibres, then jumped on to the deck of the *Marie Lamont*. Her heart was pounding with excitement. Steve moved the yacht slowly away from the pontoon. Liz, elated, stood silently watching him but he turned towards her impatiently. 'Well,' he said, 'come on. Get the fenders in.' Something else she should have known. Get the fenders in. It was all very well to read books but this was the real thing. She gave herself a little shake. You can do it, she thought. You must.

'There,' Steve pointed at the fenders that had been tied along the side of the boat to fend her off from the pontoon. Liz hauled them up on to the deck. 'Don't leave them there,' said Steve. 'Untie them and put them in that locker.'

She did as she was told, very nervous again. What on earth had possessed her to tell him she could sail?

She had thought that it would be easy enough to pretend. After all, she knew all about it in theory. It was just that everything was so new and strange and not like the books at all.

'So what do I call you?' He gave her a sidelong knowing look.

'Liz. Or Lizzie if you like.' This was a great favour although he didn't know it.

'OK Lizzie.' He was moving the *Marie Lamont* out into the bay, under engine power.

'Can I do anything else?' she asked.

He shook his head. 'Not yet. Just relax.'

Liz sat beside him in the cockpit. She was full of conflicting emotions that almost detracted from the pleasure of the moment: admiration for him as she watched his capable hands at the wheel, anger at herself, fear too.

Tom arrived at the marina just too late. He walked down to the very last pontoon, the visitor's berth, and saw the *Marie Lamont* moving smoothly out to sea. He could just make out the two figures on deck. So she really had gone. She hadn't made it up after all. He wandered up to his father's boatyard, slouching miserably, hands in pockets and sat there to wait.

When they were far enough from the shore, Steve switched off the engine and ran up some sail. 'Quiet, isn't it?' He grinned. He always loved this moment when the engine was stilled and the yacht began to move with the wind: the moment of sudden quietness when the sound of the sea itself became apparent. It never palled for him, never grew stale.

Liz watched the waves gentling the side of the boat.

Then Steve began to point things out to her. 'Now the beauty of this boat is that you can control everything from the cockpit,' he told her. 'No scrambling about the deck.'

'No.' Liz couldn't think of anything suitably intelligent or rele-

34

vent to say. Her heart sank. 'Why am I so stupid?' she thought.

'Safe in bad weather,' went on Steve. 'Great for single handing. No boom so you won't have to worry about getting your head knocked off when we gybe. Unstayed masts. No tuning.' The words flowed over Liz's head in a meaningless stream. She should understand all this but she didn't.

'So what sort of boat do you usually sail?' Steve asked her casually.

Liz hesitated. She knew that she should have been honest from the start. So absorbed was she in her own increasing misery that she didn't hear the teasing note enter his voice. 'How much have you done?' he asked. 'How are you with sail changes, that sort of thing. You don't have to do that here you see.' She wished only for the waves to part like the Red Sea and swallow them up, boat and all.

'I — I don't know.' She was thoroughly confused. 'I don't know. I don't remember.' It was like school. Worse than school. Why ever had she come?

'Oh come on now. How long ago did you sail?' Steve was brusque. 'Last season?'

Liz was still lost for words. 'Maybe,' she said. 'I don't quite. . .' Her voice trailed away. Steve sat down. The boat was slopping about gently. In irons. She remembered that. 'In irons.' The wind out of the sails. She bent her head and would not look at him, trying to hide her burning face beneath the curtains of hair.

'Sit down,' said Steve. 'Here beside me.' His tone was more gentle. He felt very sorry for her. She sat, but still she could not bring herself to look at him. 'Look. Let's get something straight. You've never done any sailing at all, have you?'

Pointless to lie, so she said nothing. Steve reached across and tilted her chin so that she was forced to look up at him. He saw raw embarrassment in her eyes, but something else; some haunting, haunted quality. He was taken aback. It was as though a screen had been briefly raised showing — what? Such a depth of misery and longing and hatred. Yes, certainly he had glimpsed a flash of pure hatred. Then it was gone and she was a sad child, caught out in a lie. 'Have you sailed?' he persisted. 'Have you?'

She jerked her head away, almost in tears. She could feel them behind her eyes, threatening to spill over, ignominiously. She never cried, or at least not where she could be seen.

'Come on kid,' he said. 'Admit it.' She looked up at him fearfully. He put his hand on her shoulder.

35

'Not much,' she said.

'You've never sailed.' It was more of a statement than a question.

'No. No I haven't.'

'That's sad.' Steve spoke lightly now that the admission was made. 'But there's no need to lie about it.'

'There is.' Liz was suddenly fierce. Steve looked hard at her and she subsided again. 'Oh I'm sorry,' she said.

'So why did you say you had, for God's sake. That could have been dangerous.'

'I thought you wouldn't take me out with you unless . . . well . . . I've read about sailing. I've read all about it. And I've watched. I thought I'd manage.'

Steve grinned. His anger seemed to have disappeared altogether. 'Lesson number one,' he said. 'There's no substitute for practical experience.'

Liz hardly dared to look at him. 'I thought you'd not take me if you knew.'

'I'm used to rookies,' said Steve. 'I teach them all the time back home.'

'Yes, but you're away from all that now, aren't you?'

She shot him a knowing look as she said this. This kid, thought Steve, is really uncannily perceptive. Sure, it had flashed through his mind. I'm away from all that. Why should I bother? He would have to watch what he thought as well as what he said. 'Look, I said I'd take you out and I will.' This time he meant it. There was something very appealing about such a fierce determination to sail. It reminded him of himself at the same age. 'You should start with a dinghy though and get the feel of being close to the water.'

'I've got a friend with a small boat. A Mirror.'

'There you are then.'

'But he only uses it for fishing.'

'Well get him to rig it. It'll be a start.'

Liz laughed. 'I doubt it. He says girls are unlucky on boats.'

'Rubbish,' Steve frowned. 'Old fisherman's tales. This is the twentieth century, I've never heard of such a thing.'

'Well that's what Tom says anyway.'

'Then he must be crazy,' Steve stood up. 'Come on. There's the breeze we're looking for. Let's get you sailing.'

At the boatyard Tom had tired of waiting. He dragged his Mirror dinghy down to the water's edge, got into it and paddled away from the shore. He loved to row around in this little boat. He could be private in his own world. This was to him what Liz's room was for her: sanctuary. Nobody could get at him here; not his father telling him what he ought to do in the boatyard and paying him peanuts for hard work, not Kate with her endless gossip and innuendo, not Jim with his fancy clothes and smart comments. Where else could he be quiet and dream of his own life, his own trawler maybe, if not out here in this little boat? Forget Liz he told himself. She doesn't care about you now so why should you care about her. But he knew that, try as he might, her image would worm its way into his head: Liz, dark haired, in a red dress, with that solemn, rather intense face which had its own peculiar beauty. 'I'll not take a lassie on a boat,' he said to nobody in particular and pulled strongly on the oars putting all his energy into the stroke.

Steve was teaching Liz to sail the *Marie Lamont*. She was clumsy at first but so eager to learn that she absorbed such information as he gave her very quickly. He had seldom encountered such a willing pupil. It was, as Steve had said, quite different from reading about it in books. It was physically so hard for one thing. 'You'll need to develop some muscles,' he told her. 'A little weight training wouldn't go amiss you know.' It wasn't easy to keep the sails taut and smooth. The boat swung alarmingly and the sails flapped loose and for the first time in her life Liz felt for herself the awesome power of wind on canvas.

Steve showed her what to do, rather than told her. 'You've got to feel how it should be,' he said. It seemed to her as though she were absorbing the very soul of the boat through her pores. The smell of it, the motion, even the taste of salt on her tongue: all were part of the experience. But it was difficult. The boat was uneasy under her hands like a horse with a new rider. 'Relax,' said Steve. 'You're trying much too hard. Taking it all too seriously girl. Relax and feel the way she ought to go. Go with it. Go with it.' He stood behind her at the wheel and placed his hands over hers. In conversations with Kate just a few weeks ago she might have giggled to think of herself in this situation. But now, although she was fully aware of him as an attractive man she saw and felt him to be a warm, capable and friendly mediator between herself and the boat. It was as if she was in tune with the boat through Steve, as if just for a moment she was absorbing his knowledge, feeling as he felt, aware of being at one with the man and the boat beneath her and with the sea through the boat. It was a kind of drowning, a way of losing oneself to the present, of being and doing rather than wishing for and hankering after. Liz had spent so long anticipating this moment that for her it was a spiritual experience. She felt at home and at peace with herself for the first time in years. The boat heeled gently, cleaving through the waves like a dolphin, fast and smooth and quiet except for the sound of rushing water against the hull, and the occasional cry of a curious gull overhead.

Tom in his rowboat saw the yacht far out in the bay, sailing. He felt desolate as he pulled for the shore. Liz, he thought. Where are you going and why can't I come too?

Steve had taken his hands from the wheel and Liz, all unawares, was on her own.

'That's right,' he said. 'You're getting the feel of it. That's good, that's good.'

His words cut into her reverie. She tensed and the boat, as if sensing it, started to move out of control.

'Watch it,' said Steve warningly. 'Watch out now.' He reached out to take the wheel again but the boat gybed violently.

Liz was crestfallen but Steve took the wheel again, laughing. 'Don't worry,' he said. 'You see, I told you, no boom to take your head off. Is there?' He glanced sideways at her. 'Make yourself useful. There's coffee below.'

Liz didn't move. She was still half lost in the moment. 'I was sailing,' she said. 'Really sailing.'

'You're not feeling sick are you?'

Liz was surprised. She had never ever thought of being sea-sick. 'No. Not at all. Why?'

'Well maybe you're the lucky one in five hundred who never is.'

'Are you ever?'

Steve shrugged. 'Only a little. If the weather's really bad. It's never stopped me sailing though. Go down and make some coffee, why don't you?'

Liz went below. The boat was spick-and-span and it was apparent that Steve had spent some of the morning tidying up after his long crossing. The hatches were open, letting in fresh air. In the galley she found instant coffee and a carton of fresh milk. She lit the gas under the kettle, put spoonsful of coffee into mugs and then took the opportunity to prowl around the rest of the boat. It was surprisingly comfortable. Beside Steve's bunk she saw a book and recognising it, picked it up while she waited for the kettle to boil. It fell open automatically at the picture of the Granny Kempock Stone. She did not notice Steve looking in at her.

'Good book eh?' he said grinning. The kettle boiled suddenly with a great crescendo of whistling steam.

'Oh sorry.' Liz made coffee and handed the two mugs up to Steve, then climbed up on deck herself.

'I expect you know a lot about local history,' he said.

'Not really but I know about the stone. The Granny Kempock Stone. We have that book at home. And Marie Lamont. I know about her.'

'Who was this Granny Kempock anyway? Why did they name a stone after her?'

Liz spilled a little coffee on to the seat beside her. Then she busied herself wiping it up with a tissue. 'Everyone around here knows about Granny Kempock,' she told him. 'She was powerful. Fishermen used to have to carry a basket of sand seven times around her.'

'Her?'

'Well — it. The stone. I don't know if there was ever a person called Granny Kempock. It's the name of the stone.'

'What about the sand?'

'For a safe voyage. And then a few years ago this guy came and tested it with a pendulum of some sort. Like dowsing you know.'

'Really?' This crazy kid believes it, thought Steve.

'Everyone thought he was a nutter. It was in the local paper. But he said he got some sort of reaction from it.'

'Did you think he was a nutter?'

Liz smiled ruefully. 'No. But then I suppose I am kind of gullible about things like that. My friends all thought he was mad. But — well — I wondered.'

Steve smiled too. She was just the sort of kid to be taken in by all that nonsense, he thought.

'So why is the stone called Granny Kempock?' he asked again.

'Nobody remembers really. They say that the real Granny Kempock was a wise old woman who could work magic. Cure you or curse you or grant your wishes. But she danced on the sabbath and was turned to stone.'

'And do you believe that?' Steve finished his coffee, throwing the dregs over the side.

'I don't know about her being turned to stone.' She turned her face away from him, towards the hill where the stone stood, a silent reminder of older beliefs, older patterns of thought. 'It doesn't really matter. I believe in Granny Kempock you see. I believe she's real. I believe she's powerful still.'

'Do you? And what of little Marie Lamont?'

Steve's voice rang oddly in her ears. Liz turned slowly to face him again. 'What do you know about her?' she asked him.

'I know what there is to know I suppose and that isn't much. Just what the guidebook says. She was accused of trying to push this Kempock stone into the sea, wasn't she? They said she was a witch.'

Liz turned back towards the shore. 'Poor Marie. Poor Marie,' she said, trying to shake off the feeling of inexpressible sadness that had come into her mind at his mention of the name; a strange, black, hopeless feeling that often invaded her head these days. Pictures came unbidden, playing themselves out in her mind's eye again like curiously vivid and intense daydreams. She saw a village street but the road was just a dirt track. There was a young girl, walking and talking with a group of women. Somehow she could see through the girl's eyes, at once a part of her and yet detached from her. They were laughing and Liz felt the mad laughter bubble up inside her too, in defiance of all those others. The others watched with suspicion. Hostile faces peered from doorways. They frowned, full of sour disapproval. On a little hillock at the end of the street was an old stone kirk. She was inside it. It was plain and chilly with bare white walls and wooden benches. She was very cold. Her feet were icy and she was clutching a shawl of coarse grey cloth about her. A minister stood lowering over her, all in black, with a big beaky nose and a frown creasing his brow. He stared down at her with sharp eyes like some bird of prey or carrion. A hoodie crow perhaps. And she was full of misery. Black misery. Why? Surely she had been laughing minutes ago?

'What's wrong?' Steve asked, breaking into her thoughts. He had seen the emotions flit uncannily across her face, and had been disturbed by them.

'Nothing,' she said. 'You broke my dream that's all.'

'What dream?'

'I was dreaming about her last night. I remember now. But why are you so interested in Marie Lamont. And why have you called your boat after her?'

'Poor Marie.' She had heard it through her dream, had said it in her dream. 'Poor Marie.'

'Well I should be interested in her. I told you she was my ancestor. That's my name. Steve Lamont. A good Scots name eh?'

He stressed the last syllable instead of, as was customary in the West of Scotland, the first. She corrected him, involuntarily. 'Lamont,' she said.

'Whatever.' He shrugged.

'You mean you're a Lamont?'

'Yes. A New World Lamont.' He still said it in his way, not hers. 'My great grandfather sailed these waters. He had a topsail schooner. She was called the *Granny Kempock*.'

'You really belong here then.' Oh Granny Kempock, how it all fits together, she thought. Aloud she asked him 'Have you seen the stone yet?'

'No. I'm aiming to though.'

'I'll show you,' said Liz eagerly. 'Oh but you're bound to be disappointed. There are houses all around it now. But I'll take you up there anyway. It's on my way home.'

'First things first.' Steve stood up. 'I thought you wanted to sail.'

'Oh I do.' Liz was happy again, her strange mood of a moment ago forgotten. Danny would scarcely have recognised her for the same girl as the sulky young creature who taunted him or ignored him in class and at home. She seemed at once younger and more mature: a nicer person altogether. 'You take me sailing,' she said, 'and I'll show you the sights. How would that be?'

'It sounds fine to me,' he said. 'Shake on it.'

He held out his hand and she took it. His skin was warm and dry, his handshake firm. She held on for a little longer than was really necessary and smiled up at him shyly. Nothing could go wrong now that he was here. He would be her protection, her anchor in the normal everyday world. With him there was surely no danger of her drifting permanently into that strange yet familiar place which haunted her dreams and her daydreams. Her mind veered away in alarm and back to Steve. 'Safe,' she thought. 'I'm safe with him.'

He felt a sudden rush of affection for this strange girl, but he removed his hand from hers. She was so young. He would have to be responsible enough for both of them.

'Tie the fenders on,' said Steve as he steered the boat skilfully back into the marina. 'Try your round turn and two hitches.' He

41

had been teaching her basic knots. 'Knitting,' he said. 'That's what you've been doing honey. Knitting, not knotting.' Then, as they came into the pontoon he taught her how to tie up the boat neatly and securely. 'When you get into port,' he told her, 'the boat is always the most important thing. That's your most valuable lesson. Before you even think of going ashore be careful that everything is just as it should be. Otherwise you'll be letting yourself in for a whole heap of trouble. Just look at the way some of these craft are tied up. It's crochet, not seamanship.' Liz thought about *Spanish Lady* and how she had airily and knowledgably shown Mr Mackenzie how to secure her with what she now knew to be a totally unsatisfactory knot. She blushed to remember it.

'Will you come up and see the stone now?' she asked to cover her confusion.

Steve hesitated, then shrugged. 'Sure,' he said. 'Why not? I'll fetch a sweater.'

As Steve and Liz were walking up through the marina Liz noticed to her intense annoyance that Tom was waiting for them. She decided to ignore him. Serve him right anyway for spying on them. 'How did I do?' she asked brightly, deliberately becoming involved in an animated conversation with Steve.

'Not bad for a first attempt. You've got enthusiasm. I'll say that for you.'

'So you'll take me out again?'

Tom stepped forward and took Liz by the arm. 'Are you not speaking then?' he asked plaintively.

Liz pretended amazement. 'I didn't see you. Didn't you go to Dunoon? With Kate?'

'No'. Tom turned and walked along beside them.

'Introduce me,' said Steve, amused, scenting jealousy.

'Oh this is Tom,' Liz spoke casually. 'He's just a friend of mine. The one I told you about, you know? Tom — this is Mr Lamont.'

'Hi Tom. Call me Steve. Lizzie does.'

'Hello.' Tom made a great effort to be polite. 'Nice to meet you. We didn't know if you were real or a figment of Liz's imagination.' Liz ignored this jibe. Steve raised his eyebrows but said nothing. They were passing Henderson's boatyard and his attention was distracted by the old wooden fishing boat.

'Liz,' he asked, 'who owns that?'

'My dad,' said Tom, brightening. Liz frowned. This wasn't what she had planned at all but Steve was full of enthusiasm. 'Your father? Lucky man! Fantastic!'

'Mr Henderson's been working on it for ages,' said Liz. Better to join in, since Steve was so obviously interested. Tom looked a little smug. 'Damn,' she thought. 'Damn him. Why must he be in on everything?'

'We worked on something similar back home,' said Steve. 'We have a little museum at our sailing school.'

'Dad's away looking at another boat just now,' said Tom, influenced in spite of himself by the casual warmth of the American. 'He charters them you know.'

'Yes. He's usually around,' said Liz valiantly struggling to keep up.

'I'd like to meet him.'

'He'll probably be tinkering with the boat on Monday. Just come up and speak to him. He'll talk about his work to anybody that'll listen. He loves it.'

'I could introduce you if you like,' Liz offered eagerly.

'No, no. I'll just go and introduce myself. I'm sure he won't mind. You tell him I'm interested Tom, will you?'

'Yes I will. Are you going home now Lizzie?'

'No.' Liz dismissed him with a wave of her hand. 'We've got something else to do. Somewhere else to go.' Go away, she thought. Leave us in peace.

'I'll go then.' Tom sounded and felt unwanted.

'Mhm. See you.'

'Bye Tom,' said the American, smiling at him sympathetically. 'This is none of my doing,' he would have said, if he could. 'Sorry about this.' He certainly felt sorry for the boy. He wondered, as Tom drifted away reluctantly, if he should have invited him to accompany them as far as the stone. Lizzie would not have been pleased, he knew that. 'Come on.' She pulled impatiently at his arm. 'Let's go. I've to be home for tea. There isn't much time. He'll be OK. He's not interested in standing stones.'

'Only in you, mm?'

'What do you mean?'

'What I say. The poor guy's head over heels.'

'Don't be daft. I've known him all my life.'

'So? What does that matter? Never heard of childhood sweethearts?'

But Liz refused to be drawn further. The hill was steep and they climbed in silence until presently they were standing beside the Kempock Stone where Liz had stood the day before, looking

43

down towards the bay. Big ragged clouds were bowling in from the West and there would be more showers before evening. Steve looked at the stone with a critical eye. 'She couldn't have done it you know.'

'Done what?'

'Pushed it over. Marie Lamont I mean.'

'No. I know she couldn't.' It was there again: a flash of raw uncontrollable rage, and then the terrible black misery descending on her. 'She was very angry, but still she couldn't do it,' she murmured.

'You know all about her don't you?' said Steve curiously.

'Of course I do.' She seemed surprised that he should ask. He watched her closely. A strange girl. She caught him staring at her and blushed.

'My gran told me about it,' she said, feeling that an explanation was required. 'She knows all the stories about the town. She used to bring me here when I was just a wee girl.' But how do I know so much, she thought. More than she ever told me. How do I remember so much? Her mind veered away, terrified and she fixed her attention on Steve, instead. 'You know — she'd tell me about Marie Lamont dancing around the stone with a coven of witches and trying to push it into the sea. And she'd tell me how if you wished on the stone your wishes would all come true.'

'And do they?'

'If you wish hard enough they do.' If you want something badly enough. If you want it day and night and never give up thinking about it and hoping and planning for it, then it'll come true. Maybe.

'Have you been wishing for anything in particular?'

'Oh yes.'

'And has it come true?'

'Maybe,' said Liz tentatively.

'What was it you wished for?'

'Oh I mustn't tell you that.'

'Why?' Steve was obviously unfamiliar with the tenuous nature of wishes.

'If I tell you then it'll all be spoilt. It'll go wrong.'

'I see.' Steve smiled ruefully. 'I guess I should try wishing for myself some time.'

'What on earth would you want to wish for?' The utter disbelief in Liz's voice amused him. She plainly couldn't imagine anything in the world that he might want. As far as she was concerned, he had it all.

'Oh plenty of things,' he said easily and then changed the subject, deliberately keeping her at arm's length.

'Maybe your grandmother would know something about my father's family,' he ventured.

'She might. She's keen on local history and she knows everyone.'

'I'd like to meet her.'

'Would you? Well there's no problem about that. She lives with us. Why not come now?'

'Should I?'

'Yes. Why not?'

'I suppose I could. Anyway if you want to go out on the boat again your parents should know. Shouldn't they?'

Liz hung her head, shamefaced, caught in a lie again. 'I suppose so.' What would he think of her?

'They must. You didn't ask them last night did you?' The casual, friendly American had disappeared and in his place was a frowning schoolteacher, too much like Danny for comfort. But more frightening than Danny, and besides, she cared what he thought about her.

'No,' she said, 'I didn't ask.'

Steve sighed. 'I guessed as much. You'll have me arrested. Listen honey we'll have to get one thing straight. If you're going to come sailing with me again you'll have to start telling me the truth.'

'I know. I'm sorry.' She paused. 'My mother's divorced. I don't see my father now.'

'Then *I'm* sorry.'

'No.' She was anxious to reassure him, always acutely sensitive to other people's discomfort even when, as with Danny, she was the deliberate cause of it. 'It doesn't matter at all. It was ages ago. But I want you to know that I don't usually tell lies. It's just that all this was so important to me. I didn't want anyone to spoil it.'

'Who would spoil it?'

'You don't understand. People don't take me seriously. They think I'm not old enough. But I am old enough to know what I want. I am!'

'Have you lied to me about that too?'

'No. I'm sixteen. I'll be seventeen at Christmas. But they don't take girls seriously you know. Just a lassie they say.'

45

Steve found it very hard to comprehend an attitude that was totally foreign to him and his upbringing. 'Nothing wrong with being a lassie,' he said seriously.

'Oh not to you maybe.' He didn't understand, that was plain to see. How could she explain to him the frustration of being rejected simply because she was a girl. 'Why should a lassie not go to sea? Why should I bide at home?' Again the words of the dream came into her mind.

Steve could see the small despairing frown beginning to crease her forehead. 'Well you're not planning to push this into the sea, are you?' he joked, gesturing at the stone.

'Not now,' she said, relaxing. 'Not now my wish has come true.'

Alice and Rose were together in the kitchen of the big flat, baking. They found it a companionable and soothing exercise. Rose had taught Alice to bake when she was still a little girl. Now they made bread and buns and pastry together once a week. Alice did the hard work and Rose lent a hand, made tea and helped to wash up afterwards. They were in the middle of jam and lemon curd tarts when Liz walked in with Steve.

Alice was still young enough to be embarrassed at having to meet a rather good looking stranger with flour and jam all over her hands but his manner was so easy and apologetic that she quickly found herself smiling at him.

'I'm sorry just to spring this on you but Lizzie tells me you won't mind.'

'He's come to meet gran,' said Liz.

'She tells me her grandmother is something of an expert on local history.'

'Oh not an expert,' Rose said, though she contrived to look flattered and pleased at the same time.

Liz decided that it was best to jump in with both feet. 'He's a sailor,' she said proudly. 'He's come all the way from America on his own. He just got in yesterday and,' this to Rose, 'he's a Lamont.'

'A Lamont?' Rose relished her role as local historian. 'Mm. A strange lot they were,' she said mysteriously.

'Well that's a good start.'

'Maybe you'd like to go through to the sitting room,' said Alice, still a little confused by his sudden arrival.

'I don't mind taking a seat just here. It's kind of cosy. And it smells just wonderful. I haven't smelled home baking in months.'

46

'Well if you're sure you don't mind.'

But Steve had already sat down on a kitchen stool, twisting his long legs around it. Rose put the kettle on again and began to slice banana bread. It was very new and crumbled under the knife.

'We heard something about your arrival last night,' said Alice. 'Local radio you know. It isn't often we get transatlantic sailors in here. Let alone single handed ones.'

'Oh I didn't want any fuss. It's no big deal. But your daughter was there, admiring my boat.'

'I do hope she hasn't been bothering you.' Liz frowned across at her mother. What a thing to say. She looked at Steve and he caught her expression of anxious pleading. 'Not at all,' he said decidedly. He could almost feel the wave of her affectionate relief engulfing him. She smiled at him: a dazzling, tender, open smile that lit up her face.

'I'm trying to find out a bit more about my family history,' he told Rose.

'Well,' said Rose modestly, 'as I said, I'm really no expert.'

'But she thinks she is,' said Steve to himself, much amused. 'And she really loves to be asked. Well, no harm in that. . .'

'You know something about the Lamonts though,' said Liz. Even after such a short time in their company Steve could see that Liz got on much better with her grandmother than with her mother. She's proud of the old girl, he thought and he remembered his own grandfather Alexander, possessed of infinitely more time and patience than his father, teaching him to sail, to navigate, to tie knots, passing on knowledge and wisdom with gentle affection. His father James had been too brusque and not really a sailor. Love of the sea had skipped a generation. Steve and his brother Alex and sister Chrissie were sailors, but his father had worked in their small town branch of a large national bank. He had done well for himself. Every weekend he had gone inland, ignoring the sea that called so insistently to his children, had gone fishing and shooting and trapping and had expected his sons at least to go along with him.

Steve's mouth twisted with distaste at the memory: the sharp unpleasant scent of fresh blood, the feel of still-warm fur and feathers, the small animals and birds sacrificed to his father's self image as Man the Hunter, providing for his family. Ludicrous, he thought, when there was a supermarket just down the road. Even as a child it had seemed crazy to him. How many times had they

47

sat at table, with Steve aged ten or eleven, red faced and sullen, refusing to eat. 'That's good food my son. Now you get that good meat down you,' his father had said grimly. Always it had ended the same way. His mother in tears, his father storming out into the garden to drink beer and himself sent up to bed without supper. Then Chrissie smuggling up peanut butter and jelly sandwiches later. But he had never given in, never once eaten the creatures his father had killed.

Alice handed him banana bread and tea. 'This stuff's American,' he told her.

'Yes. We must've known you were coming.'

The sweet, faintly astringent taste filled his mouth excising the memory of past miseries.

Alice had decided that Steve was a nice person. She divided the world into Nice People and Those Who Would Not Do. In capital letters. She couldn't understand just why this man had taken an interest in her sixteen year old daughter. Perhaps she should have been more suspicious. But she felt in her bones and in her heart that he was eminently trustworthy. A Nice Person. If he had not been, she reasoned, without any logic at all, he would not have been here, sitting on her kitchen stool, no matter that Liz was according him the kind of hero worship normally reserved for signed pictures of America's Cup and Fastnet Race winners. Alice could never understand how such oilskin muffled figures, lips so caked with salve that the individuals looked positively rabid, could arouse such enthusiasm in her daughter. She would have been happier if Liz had idolised a singer or a film star. Steve at least was real, as well as being pleasant, polite company. Any such influence was to be welcomed. She asked him to stay for dinner.

'That's very kind but I really can't impose on you.'

She could see that he very much wanted to stay. 'There's plenty,' she told him. 'I insist.'

'Well if you're sure. Thank you very much.'

Liz was positively beaming. Alice had done something right for once.

Then they heard the outer door of the flat being opened and slammed exuberantly. Danny invariably came in like a whirlwind. Alice popped the jam tarts in the oven and went out to greet him.

'My mother's boyfriend,' hissed Lizzie with a surprising amount of venom in her tone.

'Lizzie!' Rose remonstrated with her.

'Well he is, isn't he?' Liz heard her own voice ring out child-ishly. Steve shot her a surprised glance and she subsided, blush-ing furiously. Alice came back into the room with Danny. He had been jogging and coming into the warm kitchen, pink and breathless, immediately felt at a disadvantage to the cool and rather laconic Steve. Alice noticed the contrast but it only endeared Danny to her the more, which is perhaps one of the signs of true love. Infatuation does not notice flaws. Love does, but accepts them. Liz who was by no means in love with Danny immediately despised him for his appearance. Just look at him, she thought. Like a beetroot. And sweating all over the kitchen. It's disgusting.

Danny hovered uneasily in the doorway.

'This is Steve Lamont,' said Alice. 'He's an American yachts-man, come to see mother.'

'Oh aye?' Danny nodded somewhat curtly in Steve's direc-tion.'Hello.'

'Hi.'

Steve offered a handshake which Danny accepted though there was something of hostility in the grip.

'Liz brought him. He's sailed across the Atlantic.'

Danny raised scornful eyebrows. 'Everyone's doing it these days aren't they? Must be getting like Piccadilly Circus out there.'

Steve rose smoothly to the occasion if not the taunt. 'Well I'm not planning to write yet another book if that's what you mean,' he said mildly. 'But if it comes to that everybody seems to be jog-ging these days. Even I do a little back home sometimes.'

'It's no good unless you do it every day.'

'I gather it's walking that's the in thing back home. Fast walk-ing in designer trainers and tracksuit, you know?'

'That sounds more my style,' said Alice with a giggle.

Danny grunted.

'He's staying to dinner,' said Alice, anxious to placate and wondering wearily why men so often growled at each other like suspicious dogs. At least Danny did. Sometimes, while listening to conversations between him and his so called friends, she thought that they were not conversations at all but dual and intensely competitive monologues. Steve seemed a little more civilised.

'Good,' said Danny abruptly. 'You'll excuse me while I have a shower.'

49

'Don't be long,' Alice called after him.

Steve wondered if this relationship between Danny and Alice was perhaps the cause of Liz's trouble. For surely she was troubled by something.

'Your daughter wanted to know if I could give her some sailing lessons,' he said, sure that it was better to ask while Danny was out of the room.

'You have been pestering, haven't you?' said Alice to Liz.

'I don't pester.' Liz was indignant.

'Oh I don't mind,' said Steve. 'I teach sailing back home, anyway.'

'Well don't let her get in your way and don't listen to her stories.'

What stories, wondered Steve. Danny came back into the kitchen in search of a towel. He found one in a cupboard behind the door. 'He's been listening,' thought Liz, 'and now he wants to spoil it all.'

'You'll be taking your life into your hands taking her out,' was all he said and then went into the bathroom and turned on the shower, singing loudly and tunelessly over the noise of the water. Steve felt embarrassed: for Danny, for Alice, so obviously fond of him, but most of all for Liz. She was staring straight at the kitchen door. He was unprepared for what he saw when he intercepted her gaze. Her eyes were full of such black hatred that he felt his flesh creep, his scalp tingle. Am I really seeing this, he wondered uneasily?

'What's wrang wi' a woman on a boat?' came the voice, low and intense.

'Lizzie?' Alice turned to her daughter, recognising the words of the dream. But Liz was gone like a whirlwind, out of the kitchen and into her own room, slamming the door firmly shut behind her.

MARIE: 1662

It wasn't too long before things began to go wrong for me. All the folk of the village said Thomas mustn't take me on his boat. It was ill-luckit, they said, to have a slip of a lassie at the sea. Worse nor a sweep or the minister or a red headed woman. Aye well, he still took me a few times after that but then the men began to murmur that it was all wrong and harm would come of it and they wouldn't go to the fishing with Thomas any more. The folk would give me black looks in the street and only Kettie Scott and her cronies would talk to me and they were my ain mither's age and besides no fit company for a lassie like me, my faither said.

Well soon after that, my mither died and the minister stood up in the kirk and spoke angrily of superstition and sic like things but he said too that it was not seemly for a lassie to go out on a boat and like as not my mither had died of the shame of it when I knew all along that she had been coughing blood for months before.

So then Thomas, who was feart of the minister, wouldn't take me out on the boat any more. He was not a lad of great courage. We quarrelled over that and over Kettie Scott too. I said she was a good friend to me but he disagreed and then he said he wouldn't marry me either for 'twould be wrong to marry his cousin though we were not close cousins at all. And then folk said he was walking out with Janet Mackenzie of Gourock and I saw him kiss her one night down at the harbour. They were standing in the shadow of the poles where the nets are hung up to dry. They thought no-one was watching but I was. My faither said I must go into service and that he had got me a position up at Ardgowan and I must go up there and wash pots and pans, for if I could not get myself a husband I must make myself useful in some other way. He could not feed me and clothe me for ever he said, a great lump of a lassie like me.

And I was very unhappy, so I was, having no-one and nothing and not able even to go out in a boat.

It was growing late and the sun was descending through a high bank of clouds throwing a diffused angry glare into the evening sky when Tom walked alongside the *Marie Lamont*. He had lost track of Lizzie some time ago and could only imagine that she might have come back to the boat with Steve. 'Liz,' he called, hopefully, but the boat was locked up and obviously quite empty. 'Lizzie!' There was no reply. His father, walking along the pontoon, caught sight of him. 'Tom,' he called sharply, 'What are you up to now?'

'Nothing.' Recently Tom had taken to muttering at, rather than speaking directly to his father. It exasperated Mr Henderson. So did the boy's hankering after 'that terrible Liz Finlay,' as Mr Henderson called her in his own mind.

'Where've you been?' he asked sharply, sure that Tom had been following Liz around.

'Nowhere much.' Tom's voice was surly, daring his father to question him further. Henderson chose a more aggressive stance. 'Skiving off eh? I got back early. You should have been working at the yard,' he said.

'It's Saturday.'

'Whoever told you the charter business was a Monday to Friday job, mm?'

'I've got to have some time off.'

'Aye. And I'll tell you when. Get home to your tea now.' He moved on.

I could be seven, not seventeen, thought Tom, the way he speaks to me. He took another disappointed look at the deserted *Marie Lamont*, then walked after his father.

At the Finlays' flat coffee was being served to round off a good meal. Steve felt more mellow and sated than he had for months. Liz was pouring him a second cup. The introduction of a stranger into the tight little family circle seemed to have a relaxing effect on all but Danny whose conversation still bordered on hostility. Liz had come out of her room in time for the meal. It was Steve who had summoned her. He had not wanted to intrude on a family row but they had expected it of him. So he had gone to her door and called her, matter-of-factly. 'Lizzie, are you coming to eat with us or do you want a tray sent in?' Sheepishly, she had come out and taken her place at table without a murmur.

Now she seemed much happier but still she tensed every time Danny spoke. He put down his coffee cup and gave a polite little belch. 'Excuse me,' he said. Liz squirmed with dislike. He turned to Steve. 'Come looking for your roots have you?' he asked aggressively as he stretched out in the best chair. Steve did not rise to the bait. 'Sort of,' he said with a grin.'Well to be honest with you, I've come looking for a boat.'

His calm, good natured amusement riled Danny more than he cared to admit. It was a stance he was continually aiming for but never quite achieving. It seemed to come naturally to Steve.

'Another boat?' asked Rose.

'Ah but this is a very special one.'

'His family came from round here years ago,' put in Liz, anxious to display her knowledge in front of Danny.

'And how much do you know about them?' Rose was curious.

'I know my great grandfather had a little trading smack. Or shares in one. He must have done pretty well because then he became skipper owner of a small schooner.'

'Into the big time eh?' Danny was interested in spite of himself.

'Oh not that big. It loaded just over a hundred tons. Seems to have been pretty profitable though. Traded between here and the East Coast of the States. And it was called the *Granny Kempock*.' Liz drew in her breath sharply. 'You never told me that.'

'Well all we've got now is an old chunk of rock up on the hill there,' said Danny with a laugh.

'And was your great grandfather the one that emigrated?' asked Rose.

'Yes. Robert Lamont was his name. When steam came along he left for the States. I think that was at the turn of the century. I'm trying to find out a bit more about our family. But — well —,' he hesitated — 'I'm kind of hoping to find the ship as well, if that doesn't sound too dumb.'

So saying, he pulled a photograph from his pocket, and passed it round the little group. It was a black and white snapshot from the fifties: a small faded picture of an old topsail schooner. The name *Granny Kempock* was only just visible.

'But she's not likely to be around now, surely,' said Danny. 'There can't be many of these craft left. I thought most of them

53

were broken up before all these fancy conservation ideas came in.'

'So they were,' said Steve sadly, 'But it isn't just as crazy as it sounds, you know.'

'How do you mean?'

'Well a few years ago somebody brought a whole bunch of photographs into our museum office. We have a sail training school back home — a family business — and a small museum on site. My brother and sister and I set it up. Well — they run it. I teach sometimes and bum around when I can't stand it any more. Anyway there were a lot of pictures of the Clyde and some of them were quite recent. Among them was this one of an old top-sail schooner called the *Granny Kempock*. It looks as if she was being used as a yacht at that time. The donor said they'd been taken by his father in the late fifties but his father was a sailor himself and it's difficult to say where this was taken. But the fifties — well I mean she could've survived. God knows where. She'd make a great sail trainer for our school. Especially if she'd been well converted. If she's still around I want to find her.'

'Another *Marie Lamont* and now a *Granny Kempock*.' Liz looked long and hard at the photo. 'She's lovely,' she said finally. 'You must talk to Tom's dad. He might know something about her.'

'So you really do teach sailing?' asked Alice. She had been only half convinced.

'Oh yes. We're primarily a sailing school. We just run the museum on the side. My grandfather made quite a bit of money at the sea. My father went into banking. The nautical bit skipped a generation . . . came out in all three of his children. My sister too,' he said, with a glance at Liz. 'Poor guy. We spent his money and his father's money too, on the school.'

'And you're going to teach me aren't you?' asked Liz eagerly.

Steve turned from Alice to Danny. A little tact was called for here. But why was he going to so much trouble for this particular kid? Because for her it was so important. A matter of life and death. He stopped short. Why had that thought come into his head? Important yes, but life and death? Perhaps her sense of melodrama had communicated itself to him. He smiled at Alice and Danny. 'If you'll allow it.' He looked directly at Danny. 'Sure — she can do some sailing with me for a few days.'

Liz held her breath. Please Granny Kempock, please.

'You'll have your hands full,' said Danny. His cynicism

angered Rose and Liz. Even Alice was irritated by it though to a lesser degree. 'I find it impossible to teach our Lizzie anything and I'm a professional.'

'I'm not your Lizzie,' said Liz furiously.

'Now Elizabeth.' Keep the peace at all costs thought Rose.

'I'm a professional too you know, in my own way,' said Steve. He found himself disliking Danny enormously but then he had to remind himself that the poor guy probably knew Liz a hell of a lot better than he did.

'That's very kind of you,' said Alice to Steve. 'I'm sure Liz will be very grateful.'

Liz breathed a sigh of relief. 'Come and see the dragon,' she said to Steve as though she were conferring a great favour on him.

'The dragon?'

'Her lizard.' Danny pulled a face and Liz scowled back at him.

'It's her pet lizard,' said Rose. 'Danny hates it.'

'Well it smells,' said Danny.

'No it doesn't,' said Alice. 'You never see it so you wouldn't know. It doesn't smell.'

'No.' Liz rounded on him. 'It's private. I don't show it to just everyone. It's special.' She dazzled Steve with her smile. 'Come on and I'll show you.'

Steve got up, rather reluctantly. Danny raised his shoulders, dismissing the matter. 'Good luck to you.'

Steve followed Liz into her room. It astonished him though on reflection he wondered why. Surely he should have expected it: this obsession with sailing and the sea. But he had a kid sister who was keen on sailing and even her bedroom had never ever looked like this. This was so full of nautical objects and pictures that you could almost taste the salt on your tongue. He could hardly take it all in. He loved the whalebone carving. 'This is beautiful, just beautiful,' he kept saying, picking it up to look more closely at it.

'Here he is.' She summoned him and he peered down into the heated tank.

'Good God,' he said. The little creature stared back at him with bright lidless eyes.

'My dragon,' said Liz.

'My God,' said Steve again.

She took the little creature out of its tank. It sat unafraid on her hand. 'Here — you can hold it if you want to.'

55

Steve sensed that this was a very great privilege. 'Are you sure?' he asked, surveying the lizard doubtfully.

'Yes. Go on.'

Steve took the lizard on his hand and tried to outstare it. It stared back at him, unblinking.

'It isn't everyone that can handle him,' said Liz. 'And he objects to some people. Tom for instance. And I wouldn't let Danny touch him.'

Steve grinned at her. 'Perhaps he wouldn't want to.'

'He says not.'

He looked sidelong at her, keeping his attention on the lizard. 'You're hard on poor old Danny aren't you?'

'Poor?' she demanded. 'Why poor?' One minute she was a child, the next a woman. 'He's hard on me. He's always on at me.' She was very indignant. 'Anyway never mind about Danny. Don't you like him?' She nodded at the lizard.

'I'm sure I could soon grow to love him. He isn't everyone's idea of a pet though.'

'My familiar,' she said the word under her breath. It was a key. Smoothly it unlocked a door in her mind. She was elsewhere. In a small room crammed with people, all women, all older than she. There was a reek of peat smoke and a smell of new bread, a good wholesome smell. She was just a lassie. She was their foolish wee lassie. A great surge of affection welled up inside her. They mothered her. She had no mother now and they knew and so they loved her, petted her, made much of her. But who was this now, and why were the women half afraid, half excited? A tall dark man came in through the door, stooping a little because of his height. He held out his hands to her. They were beautiful, smooth, white hands with the nails neatly cut, the hands of a man who had never in all his life worked, neither at the farming nor the fishing. Not like her own Thomas. Thomas's hands had been brown and scarred, the nails dirty. When he had touched her cheek she had been able to smell fish. She took the stranger's hands and he squeezed her fingers, her own red rough fingers with the nails all ragged from the soapy water in the scullery at Ardgowan. And then he released her, only to pull her closer and hold her there for a second in his embrace. Her face was against his breast-bone. She could hear his heart beating. 'My sister,' he said. His arms were wiry and very strong. Like Steve, she thought. The door in her mind slammed shut again. She looked up. Steve was smiling down at her. She looked at his hands holding the lizard. His fingers were long and strong and brown, not smooth and white. But she wondered what it would be like to be held in his arms. Foolish, she thought. A foolish wee lassie.

'Your what?' Steve was asking.

'My familiar spirit. Like witches have.'

'I see.'

'More exciting than a cat. I tell him everything. He knows all about me. He's magic.'

'I think maybe he ought to go back into his tank.'

'Yes. OK.' She took the little creature tenderly on to her hand. 'Come on dragon.' She returned him gently to his home.

'So he knows all your secrets does he?'

'Yes. All of them. All of Marie's secrets.'

'Sorry?' What on earth was she talking about?

'All of my secrets.'

What fantasy was this, thought Steve? She was staring dreamily at the lizard again. But what was she really seeing? What caused that sudden darkening of her eyes so that they looked as cold and unblinking as those of her Dragon, her familiar. He shivered involuntarily, 'Let's go back to the others,' he said uneasily, wanting to get out of the room, wanting, in a way that was quite foreign to him, company, warmth and normality.

Later that evening Alice, Danny and Rose sat up in the sitting room finishing a bottle of wine and discussing Liz. Steve had departed for his boat carrying a large tin of Alice's home made cakes. Liz had gone to bed exhausted by the day's happenings. They seemed to spend far too much time discussing Liz as though she were some great insurmountable problem rather than a flesh and blood girl only just emerging from childhood. Danny resented it.

'She's sensitive,' said Rose defensively. But then she always defended Liz no matter what, always sided with her against himself, thought Danny.

'Maybe so, but it's beginning to get out of hand,' he said.

'I think,' said Alice with the air of one dropping a bombshell, 'I think that she really doesn't want to go back to school after the holidays. I don't think it was a joke when she mentioned it. I think she's not going to go.'

'Is she crazy or what?' Danny nearly choked on his drink. The wine was supposed to be making the conversation easier.

'What on earth would she do?' he asked.

'Get a job.'

'Oh yes. There's plenty of those around here I suppose. What kind of job? A boat cleaner maybe?'

'Don't be silly.' That was Rose again.

'Well it's just about all she's qualified for.'

'Danny's right, mother.'

'Anyway it's just a pose. She will go back. I'll speak to her.' Rose sounded more sure than she felt. Sometimes her patience infuriated Danny. He was a volatile individual: quick to anger but just as quick to forgive and forget. Liz's capacity for bearing grudges constantly amazed and disgusted him. 'Anyway it doesn't surprise me,' he said. 'She doesn't want to learn. I've tried, believe me. But she's always in a dream somewhere.' He was a conscientious teacher and hated to fail.

'We'll have to wake her up somehow,' said Alice.

'That's easier said than done,' thought Danny but he said nothing.

'We'll have to make her see sense. Grow up,' Alice continued.

'Oh there's nothing wrong with being a dreamer,' Rose spoke easily, reassuringly. She almost convinced Alice, if not herself. 'A bit of escape. That's what a girl needs. Can't you see that? A bit of escape.'

Late Monday morning found Steve at Bill Henderson's boatyard watching admiringly as Henderson worked on his boat. The day was overcast and there was rain on the wind. Tom was helping his father. He liked to work with wood, liked the feel of it beneath his fingers. The old sailing smack held pride of place in the yard propped up on great wooden blocks. There was a ladder leaning against the boat. Tom worked away up on deck while his father came down to talk to Steve.

'Hoping to charter her?' asked Steve.

'One of these days.' Henderson patted the old boat, lovingly. 'Ach it's getting the timber right. I'm beginning to regret it a bit already. It's a full time job and I just don't have the hours.'

'Beautiful though.' Steve could not resist old boats. Each had its own peculiar personality. To see something that had survived in all the beauty of its craftsmanship, no matter how decayed, gave him a thrill of pure excitement. He couldn't bear to see old boats left to rot, broken up, sunk. More than once his family had rescued an old craft to regret it later during the hours of hard work such renovation entailed.

'And the expense,' said Henderson. 'My God the expense.'

'Like burning dollars,' Steve agreed. But it was always worth it. Always. In his heart, Henderson agreed. 'She's beautiful,' said Steve, 'isn't she?' He gave the boat another little pat. 'Mind you that's the worst of wooden boats. You're never done with them. Fibreglass is a lot easier.'

'Ever tried a concrete boat?' Henderson went back to work but carried on talking. 'Tom — hand me down that hammer.'

'I've sailed in one.They're OK. Very tender though. Need a strong stomach. They only stiffen up in a force seven or eight.'

Henderson laughed. 'They tell me you've to carry a bag of readimix and a roll of chicken wire in case of accidents.'

'That's about it.' Both men enjoyed the joke, recognising a shared interest and liking each other for it. Tom, who had heard the comment many times before pulled a face, but not so that his father could see him.

Liz stood in the gateway of the yard watching them. They did not notice her there, but as she saw them laughing together, a curiously jealous, hurt expression crossed her face.

'They're laughing at me,' she thought. 'They don't need me. They can do without me. Tom's dad'll be telling Steve I'm crazy. He'll believe him. Men always believe each other. They must be laughing at me. I hate them all.'

She stood, poised there, unsure whether she should walk in or go away. Her first impulse on seeing them together had been to run but she had managed to resist it.

'So you run a sailing school back home do you?' she heard Bill Henderson say to Steve.

'Yeah. We do a bit of charter work too. Risky business.'

Bill Henderson smiled sympathetically. 'There's some real wallies about,' he agreed. 'They block the bogs with fag ends, they run down the batteries and they run out of fuel and if there's a brick to run aground on you can guarantee they'll find it.'

'That's just about it,' said Steve. 'I wonder — do you ever come across any of the old sailing schooners on this coast?'

Henderson shrugged. 'Not really. Not any more. Not unless they've been done up as luxury yachts.'

'This one was I think.'

'Which one?' Henderson was interested.

'A little topsail schooner. She was called the *Granny Kempock*.'

Henderson frowned. 'There's a wee fishing boat by that name.'

'Oh this one was steel. Built in the 1890s. In Greenock I think.'

'I'll ask around,' said Henderson. 'I doubt it though.'

'Well thanks anyway. I'd be grateful,' said Steve. He turned around to see Liz watching him. He had felt her gaze boring into his back. 'Hi,' he said cheerfully. How long had she been standing there watching with that fixed intense expression. What was wrong with the girl for God's sake?

'Hi.' She was very distant. 'Hello Tom.'

Henderson wiped his hands on a piece of cloth and went over to look in his toolbox. 'How are you Eizabeth?'

She gave him a thin smile. 'I'm fine thank you Mr Henderson.' She looked up at the boat. 'Isn't she beautiful?' Liz was almost unnaturally taken with the boat. She seemed fascinated by it, patting and stroking the wood with little delicate rhythmic movements.

'She is lovely, isn't she?' said Tom.

'Are you interested in sailing too Tom?' asked Steve. Liz, her attention still riveted on the boat, answered for him. 'No,' she said, a little contemptuously. 'He just paddles around the harbour. I told you.'

'He's into fishing,' said Henderson. 'He'd like to run away on a trawler wouldn't you, eh Tom?'

'You know how I feel about the fishing,' said Tom seriously and then to Steve. 'I've done a bit of dinghy sailing. Not much though.' He was very anxious to please Liz but she ignored him.

'Are we going out today?' she asked Steve cautiously.

'If you like. The weather's not too good but I don't mind a little rain if you don't. I've got a bit of work to do on the engine first though. And we need water.'

'I'll do that.'

'I could give you a hand.' That was Tom. Bill Henderson frowned. 'What about your work son?'

'Can I not have a wee break?'

'I don't need a hand,' said Liz firmly. 'I can do it. Besides, I know what you think about girls on boats.'

Steve threw her the keys of the *Marie Lamont*. 'Catch. I'll be down in a minute.' Liz could hardly believe it. He had actually trusted her with the keys to his boat. So perhaps he and Tom's father hadn't been laughing at her after all. Perhaps it had been something quite different. I must be going daft, she thought. Why am I so suspicious of people all of a sudden? Why do I feel that I can't trust anybody? I must trust somebody so why not Steve? Steve was smiling at her. It was as though the sun had come out.

She went off briskly down the pontoon, whistling cheerfully, thumbs in the pockets of her jeans.

'What's all this about girls on boats?' asked Steve. 'She keeps going on about it.'

'I used to tell her it was unlucky.' The boy looked at his father sheepishly. 'It was a bit of a laugh but she took me seriously. She's never let me forget it.'

'That was when he wasn't keen on girls messing up his fishing trips,' said Henderson winking at Steve.

'Can I have a break dad?' Henderson nodded grudgingly. 'Go to the office and put the kettle on. We'll have lunch. I'll be up in a minute.' Tom drifted away.

'Now he's not so sure,' said Henderson to Steve after Tom had gone. 'About lassies on boats I mean. He fancies her. I wish he didn't.'

'Why?'

Henderson didn't answer at first but just carried on working. Presently however he said, 'So young Elizabeth's attached herself to you has she?'

'That's just about it.'

'She's a wee pest.' Bill felt badly for his son. Liz was to blame, leading the boy on and then dropping him flat. 'Always hanging about the marina.' Steve was taken aback by the man's virulence. He wondered why Liz aroused such antagonism in men like Bill and Danny. What had Bill and Danny in common that Liz should make them feel so uncomfortable?

'And the tales she tells,' said Henderson. 'Don't believe a word of any of them. Don't believe anything she tells you.'

Steve wasn't inclined to argue. 'I'll cope,' he said, laconically, but Henderson fired a parting shot after the American as he left. 'I'm telling you, you'll never be rid of her now,' he said. 'Never.'

Liz and Steve sat in the cockpit of the *Marie Lamont*. Cloud had descended from the hills muffling sea and shore in a white wet blanket. Though there was no obvious rain, the air itself had drenched hair and clothes. 'This what you call Scotch mist?' asked Steve, pulling a face.

'I suppose so.' Steve was tinkering with the engine while Liz fidgeted next to him. 'For God's sake sit still,' he said finally. 'What's the matter? Got ants in your pants?' She folded her arms and crossed her legs stilling herself with an effort.

'I did it all right?' she asked finally. 'The water? I did it all right didn't I?'

'If it's coming out of the taps you did it right.' Steve refused to praise her for something so simple. 'Do you know if I can get a train to Glasgow on Wednesday morning? Early?'

'They run pretty often.'

'I have to do a bit of research. And I've been invited to lunch.' He was very offhand.

'There's one at half past eight I think.'

Liz paused. 'Hey,' — a wonderful idea — 'I could come with you. Show you where everything is.' Surely he had been going to ask her anyway.

'No,' said Steve, very firmly. Then, as if to refute further argument 'Here — give me that cloth. Let's get this finished.'

'Then we can go?'

'Oh I don't know.' He looked up at the sky. 'Visibility's nil out there. In here too for that matter. You'd have to plot a course just to get to Dunoon today.' He saw the disappointment in her face. 'But the forecast is good. We'll sit it out for a bit. See what happens.' He began to wipe his oily hands. She watched the strong capable fingers.

I love you, she thought. I'm sixteen and I love your boat but I think I love you too. It's the first time. How could she tell him. What could she say? How silly she would sound if she tried to put any of this into words.

'I've nothing to do this week,' she said plaintively. 'Are you quite sure I can't come and help you?'

'Quite sure,' said Steve. And that was final, his tone implied.

'I see,' said Liz. He looked sidelong at her disappointed face, sorry for her in spite of himself. 'Cheer up,' he said. 'We'll take her out just as soon as the mist clears. OK?'

She gave him a watery smile in return.

Alice was all dressed up and ready to go out for lunch with Danny. She looked at herself in a wall mirror, brushed her hair and applied fresh lipstick and scent. She was a pretty woman and some of her quick nervous movements were very much like her daughter's. Rose watched her anxiously.

'Alice — you should tell Elizabeth yourself,' she said firmly, even sternly. 'You shouldn't be leaving it to Danny of all people.'

'Why of all people?' Alice whirled on her and again Rose saw Liz in the quick tempered movement.

'You must be blind if you can't see how she feels about him,

62

Alice. Oh I like him well enough. Don't start getting at me. It isn't my fault. His bark's worse than his bite, I can see that. But she can't. He's her teacher, she dislikes him and she dislikes what he teaches and that's all she can think about just now.'

Alice sighed, admitting the truth of this.

'Perhaps she'd take it better coming from you.'

'No. You're her mother. You tell her.'

'But you're closer to her. She talks to you. She'll tell you how she really feels about us.' Alice looked at her watch. 'Oh God I do wish he'd hurry up.'

'Why? Because your daughter might be back?'

'No. Anyway she's on the boat with Steve. She won't be back yet. Not for hours.'

'Don't worry.' Rose looked at Alice through the mirror, impatient with her. 'And stop fiddling about will you?'

She could never understand Alice's obsession with her appearance; with her hair, her nails, her make-up and her figure. Alice was positively thin, yet always maintained that she was at least a stone overweight. 'At least a stone,' she would say, over and over again, to Rose's intense annoyance. Thank God Liz hadn't inherited this same concern.

'He'll be here,' said Rose. 'He never fails.' She paused. Now was as good a time as any. The right moment would never come. 'The thing is — I don't know how much longer I'll be here, Alice.' Badly put, she thought, as Alice turned a shocked face towards her.

'What on earth do you mean?' she asked. 'Are you ill? What's the matter with you?' Her voice was filled with panic.

'No, no.' Rose put a reassuring arm around her. 'I'm not ill. But I mean I won't always be here. After you're married again. I've been looking at some nice wee flats. I think I might have seen one I like.' She had been to look at a quiet sheltered housing development and seen a beautifully decorated little flat which she could just afford. There was enough room for her possessions. It was sunny and light with central heating and even a window box. There was a lovely communal garden to sit in too, well maintained by a gardener. The flat would fall vacant in a couple of months time when the present tenant went to live with her son. Rose would have to make the decision within a few weeks. But if she admitted it, she had already decided. Her heart had already gone out to the little flat. She wanted it badly, wanted the freedom it would give her to entertain her friends, to go to bed late at nights and to sleep in, in the mornings, to drink strong black coffee at suppertime and even the odd whisky without her daughter worrying about her. In some ways, she thought, age was like adolescence all over again. The thought of freedom excited her as much as her first independent home had. She remembered the little house she and her husband had first rented: lace curtains at the windows and a kitchen like a shoebox. But it had been paradise. Now, she found herself recapturing that feeling. No wonder she understood Liz so well, understood that first acute desire for independence.

Alice broke in on her thoughts.

'You can't live on your own.' She was horrified. 'And besides there's no need. Danny's moving in here you know.'

'Yes but you and Danny will need more room.'

'There's plenty of room for you here. I just assumed. . . .'

Rose cut her short. 'Well don't,' she said though not unkindly. 'Don't assume anything Alice.'

Outside they heard the sound of Danny's 'Colonel Bogie' car horn. Alice leaped as if she had been stung, gathering together coat and bag.

'Listen,' she said. 'We'll talk about this later.'

'If you like.' Rose's shrug meant that whatever was said, nothing would change her mind. Her stubbornness reminded Alice of Liz.

'You've spoiled my lunch now,' she said sulkily.

'Don't be silly. Just think about it. You'll see it from my point of view, I know. Besides — it's what I want. You're doing what you want, aren't you Alice? Why expect me to be any different?'

'Oh mum,' said Alice, changing the subject. 'Talk to Elizabeth will you? I can't.'

Rose relented a little as Alice had known she would. 'I'll try.'

'But don't say anything about moving out yet,' said Alice urgently at the door. 'Please. Not yet. Will you?' Rose went out into the hallway with her daughter. 'Off you go,' she said. 'He'll be waiting for you. I'll keep quiet for now.'

'Help me tell her,' said Alice.

Rose almost pushed her out of the door. 'I'll see what I can do, but I'm not promising anything.'

Danny was leaning on the horn as Alice came out of the door. She scrambled into the car. 'Hush,' she said, 'the neighbours will be furious.' But she loved him for his assumed imperiousness. She kissed him on the cheek. 'What kept you?' he asked, accelerating away.

The cloud had descended further and the *Marie Lamont* was completely smothered in mist. The marina buildings had all but disappeared; only one or two masts and blurred hulls loomed out nearby like ghost craft, but in the cockpit they were quite alone, shrouded and shut in together, the two of them. Even their voices were a little deadened by the cold pall of moisture, and when she looked at Steve's face it seemed to her as though the chill in the air had somehow milked the colour from it leaving it pale and haggard.

Perhaps we're both ghosts, she thought. Perhaps we've died and now there's nothing else. Only this boat and the mist and the two of us. And here we'll be forever. And I hardly know him. Perhaps this is what it's like to drown. Better to drown than to burn.

'Tell me more about Marie Lamont,' he said and though the normality of his voice reassured her his question only served to reinforce her odd impression of being at one remove from reality.

'Marie,' she said dreamily. 'Poor Marie.'

'Marie Lamont, Lizzie.' Steve spoke with a sort of false heartiness. Her sudden changes of mood made him edgy and the mist was unnerving him too. 'The one who was a witch and tried to push the stone into the sea. You must know more about her.'

'Oh I do.'

'Then tell me. But let's go below. Have some lunch while we're waiting. There's sandwiches and I'll make coffee. I'm getting cold, I don't know about you.'

Below deck he put on a heater and lit lamps. He had been oddly reluctant to hear the story out there on deck encircled by that gleaming white wall. Down here, as warmth began to seep into his bones, he felt more at ease. He busied himself in setting out a simple meal.

'She was young. Not much older than me.' Liz began quietly, matter of factly, as though the story were a part of her. 'And she wanted to go to sea. Her father was a fisherman but this was 1661 you must remember. They wouldn't let her go.'

'You even know the dates.'

'Of course I do,' Liz smiled. 'Why wouldn't I?'

Was it his imagination or was her accent growing broader as she became more and more possessed by the story?

'So why wouldn't they let her go to sea?'

'Oh you know. Superstition. Women. Bad luck on boats.'

65

Steve laughed uneasily. 'There you go again. That's what Tom Henderson said, isn't it?'

'Tom Henderson?' said Liz brought briefly back to the present. 'Oh he's a pain.'

Steve began to eat. Liz took a mug of coffee and sat warming her hands around it.

'They aren't unlucky,' she said. 'They aren't.'

Steve found himself quoting her, drawn into the fantasy. 'Why should a lassie not go to sea?'

'Well people used to think it was unlucky. Anyway, the town was just a little village then. Granny Kempock — the stone — stood up on the hill. You must've been able to see her for miles around. She was a marker for the fishermen to steer by and before they set off on a long voyage they used to carry a basket of sand around her seven times, widdershins.'

'Widdershins?'

'Anti-clockwise. Against the sun. You know, when the fishermen are leaving harbour they mustn't turn the boat against the sun. It's bad. Wrong. But with Granny Kempock it was different. That was how it had to be. Widdershins. That was how you summoned the power.'

'Go on.'

'They would carry baskets of sand and wish for favourable winds. And then the girls. . . .' There was contempt in her voice now. 'The girls used to go up there and ask her for a husband.'

'Oh sure.' Steve was incredulous.

'No. Don't laugh. I told you she could grant wishes. But Marie didn't need a husband. She wanted a boat.'

'Like you,' said Steve, the light beginning to dawn. This kid was identifying with Marie Lamont. That was why his boat seemed so significant to her. She must be identifying herself with that seventeenth century girl who had also wanted to go to sea. What a load of romantic hooey he thought, relieved, and how like a sixteen year old. Liz paused and then confirmed his idea. 'She wanted to sail. More than anything else she wanted to sail.'

'Like you.'

'Anyway, one of the fisher lads in the village — he must've been in love with her because she finally made him take her out with him. And she was a good sailor. Strong. Good at the fishing too.'

'How do you know?' asked Steve lightly. 'Did you read it somewhere or do you just have a good imagination?'

66

She looked back at him blankly. 'How do I know?' She faltered. 'How do I know? Because. . . .' She stopped, unable to go on. Steve felt uneasy again.

'More coffee?' he said. She nodded, handing him her mug. When he gave it back to her she was aware of their hands briefly touching. She wondered when she had become physically so aware of him. She could not remember the exact moment but now the sense of arousal in herself confused her. She had never felt this with Tom: a spark and crackle of sensation between herself and the man, that made her heart beat faster, her skin flutter and her breath quicken. Her hand on the plastic mug was shaking. She wondered if he felt it too. Probably not, she thought. She was new to all this and the intensity of her emotional and physical response to him frightened her. Her body felt out of control. She had no means of coping with it, no previous experience with which to compare it. She could only stare up at him in mute admiration.

But he had felt it. She was sitting on a bunk close to him, her head thrown back. The cabin was warm. Her damp hair gave off a faint sweet perfume as it dried. She smelled of desire. He looked down at her and saw for a moment a woman's body, saw her craving for him in her eyes, the child quite lost beneath that dawning adult passion. Then he remembered her youth and, summoning all his willpower, moved away.

He opened the hatch and looked out. A breeze had sprung up and high above them watery sunlight was beginning to filter through. The mist was breaking up into thin veils, all rags and tatters. 'Thank God,' he thought. 'Thank God for that.'

He poked his head down. 'It's clearing,' he said. 'Let's sail.'

MARIE 1662

Well then, a year since I was at Kettie Scott's house and with me were Janet Hynman of Gourock, Margret Letch, Jean King, Margret Rankin of Greenock and some others. It was in the midst of the night and the devil was there in the likeness of a muckle dark man with black curls. He was a braw mischancie kind of a man so he was. And he sang to us and played the fiddle and we danced. He gave us wine to drink and wheat bread to eat and we were all very merry. It was Kettie first made me acquent with him and I wondered that he had the hands of a gentleman so smooth and white they were. Later he walked with me up to Ardgowan through the fields and the moon was full and yellow. I was

67

greatly feart to be my lee lane with such a one and my heart trembled within me. He said I must call him Serpent or Maister for he was my true Maister and not yon auld birkie up at Ardgowan, and then he drew me in close under the shadow of the gate and embraced me to seal the bargain. I felt his warm breath on my cheek and was like to swoon. He would have kissed me but that the house door opened just then and I was feart we might be seen. But the next day Kettie said he did me much honour and I would be a foolish lassie if I did not let him have his way with me.

4

Soon the yacht was pushing out into the Clyde under power with Steve at the controls. Liz stood like a figurehead braced against the breeze. The mist was quite gone. When they were out in the bay and sailing in light airs and strengthening sunshine Steve's curiosity reasserted itself. 'So what was the problem for Marie Lamont, if she'd got someone to take her out?' he asked. 'Sounds like a happy ending to me.'

'Oh — custom, fear, people.' Liz looked up towards the hillside. 'Why do people always spoil everything?' she asked and the depths of sadness in her voice alarmed him, filled him again with concern for her.

'You're very cynical for one so young,' he said lightly. 'Here. Hang on to this.' He made her take the wheel. 'I hate to think what you'll be like when you're my age.'

When Liz raised her head to look at him her eyes and voice were alike threatening. 'Don't laugh at me. Why do you laugh at me?'

He had laughed at her always. That other tall man who looked like Steve. Except for the hands. The long strong white fingers. Clowts, he had called her. Not a pretty name. 'Don't laugh at me,' she said. 'Don't laugh at me or. . .'

'Or you'll what?'

His voice belied the sense of foreboding he felt. The boat swerved and the sails flapped. 'Watch it,' he warned. 'Hold her steady now.'

'Or I'll. . .' she hesitated. Why was she daring to threaten him, of all people? She sighed and relaxed. 'Oh I don't know.'

Steve rested his arm lightly on her shoulders. 'I don't laugh at you Lizzie. I laugh with you. There's a difference you know. I like you too much to laugh at you.' She turned a brilliant smile on him. It was true, why did he feel relieved at her change of mood?

'Tell me more,' he said.

'Well it was unlucky to take a woman on a boat. It was unnatural, they said. I expect his family and other people kept telling him so. His friends. You know. Nobody else would go out with him while she was on board. And he wasn't strong enough. He

69

just gave in to them. Anything for a bit of peace and quiet. Like Tom.'

'What do you mean?'

'Peace and quiet. Like Tom. He wants to go to the fishing but his dad says no, so he doesn't go. He could. He's seventeen, almost eighteen. He could go if he really wanted to.'

'Do you like fishing?'

'Killing things? No. I hate it. The boat gets all bloody and it smells terrible. The fish lie there gasping. He guts them but they're alive when he does it and they're still alive after it. He says they can't feel anything but how does he know? I hate it.'

'Is Tom a part of all this too?' he asked her.

'Tom? He shouldn't have given in.'

'What?'

'He gave in to them. He shouldn't have, should he?'

Alice and Danny were driving home after a lunch that had not been entirely successful. Liz had been the main topic of conversation and Danny had acute indigestion.

'She isn't normal,' he said with sudden intensity. 'I still say it isn't normal for a girl of her age.'

Alice didn't know how to reply to this open and unexpected declaration of hostility. She looked out of the window, biting her lip. Danny drove on.

Liz was still at the wheel of the boat. 'So,' she said, 'Tom told Marie she'd have to stop coming with him. No more sailing. No more hauling in the nets full of the silver herring. No more wind in your hair and salt on your lips.'

'I thought you didn't like fishing.'

'No.' She looked at him, uncertainty in her eyes. 'But I don't know. I don't know.'

'You say Tom told Marie?'

'No,' — impatiently — 'not Tom. This fisher lad. Her cousin.'

Steve took the wheel. 'But you said. . .' He paused. 'Oh well. Never mind. Here. Let me.' Liz stood beside him, watching the sea, then spoke with an increasing passion. She had become wild eyed again, her dark hair flying in the wind. Steve realised that he found her beautiful. After the lonely voyage, his body that had long been quiescent in the pull and tug of the waves, stirred at her proximity, but he forced his mind back to his steering.

'Her father told her she'd need to go into service. He'd got her a place he said. Proper woman's work. What he meant was a skivvy. Washing the pots and pans and the dirty dishes. And what then? Clowts, they called her. Cloths. Oh she'd marry. Poor Clowts. Maybe even a fisher lad, and what then? She'd gather in the mussels in the cold dawn and bait the long lines and catch her fingers on the hooks till they were red raw and bleeding and have endless kids but never go to sea.' Her voice rang out higher and more piercing than the wind.

In Liz's room, Rose was waiting for her granddaughter to come home. She tidied up a little, though Liz kept her miscellany of possessions neat and clean, another reason why Danny found her unnatural. Then she sat on the bed and watched the lizard, stretching out her hand to it. It darted at her suddenly, making her flinch.

Aboard the *Marie Lamont* Steve noted with one part of his mind that black clouds were gathering low on the horizon while with another part he carried on listening, fascinated both by the story and by the intensity with which it was being told.

'She would have to carry her husband on her back to his boat through the shallow water so he'd not get wet. And the stones cutting her feet so that they matched her hands. Red raw and bleeding. Well that wouldn't matter — oh but never to go to sea. Never to feel the boat leaping under her. Never to know the freedom of it.'

Alarmed by the look that had again come into her eyes, the expression again of hatred, Steve reached out and touched her gently on the shoulder. 'Liz,' he said but she ignored him. She was totally locked into a world of her own, not seeing him at all. He shook her gently.

'I hate them,' she said in a low intense voice. The air around him seemed vibrant with the force of the statement. He shook his head in determined refutation.

'Yes. I hate them all.'

In the car Danny lost control of the steering. It was as though somebody had wrenched the wheel out of his grasp and turned the car violently to the right. Danny, struggling and swearing, just managed to avert a crash with an oncoming lorry. He pulled into the side of the road with a squeal of brakes. The lorry driver made a rude gesture and drove on, sweating. 'Bloody idiot,' he said to his dog on the seat beside him. The big German Shepherd looked over its shoulder, raised its hackles and curled its lip in a snarl. It growled low in its throat, ears back, then shivered and subsided.

'What the hell were you doing?' asked Alice still shaking with fright, her own scream ringing in her ears. Danny rested his head on the wheel, fighting to pull himself together. 'I don't know,' he said. 'My God I don't know what happened. I could've sworn somebody' — he groaned and shook his head. 'No. Nothing. It must have been a skid. It must.'

'I hate them all,' Liz repeated, her fists clenched, her knuckles showing very white. Steve tightened his grip on her shoulder.

Close in by the harbour, Tom was fishing from his little boat. His father, with one of his customary but inexplicable changes of heart, had let him leave early. Quite suddenly the dinghy rocked violently from side to side as though in the wash of some much larger craft, though none was visible. Tom almost fell into the water. He looked about him, surprised and alarmed, but could see no cause for this movement. After a while he settled down again but his mood of quiet concentration was shattered.

Aboard the *Marie Lamont* Liz stirred and looked directly at Steve. He relaxed his grip on her shoulder. 'She must have hated them all, mustn't she, all those people,' she said, as though nothing had happened.

'Perhaps.'

'She hated Thomas most of all. She felt betrayed by him you see. She went with her friends and tried to push the stone into the sea.'

'Why?'

'To raise stormy weather of course. To destroy a wheen fishing boats.'

The hillside was bleak and exposed. The stone loomed up out of the darkness. They danced with manic energy and it was as though their collective emotions, springing from hatred, deprivation and frustration generated some power that was quite external to them. They tried to push the stone into the sea. She remembered the feeling of intense effort. Nothing happened. Something happened. Some malevolence went winging from them and down towards the water. A wind rose and beat about their heads. They fled in terror from the blind impersonal force to which they had given will and direction.

'I suppose the old stone just stood there.' Steve forced himself to speak lightly. 'It wouldn't budge. Not magic. Just a cold old

72

stone with a heart of stone to match, eh?' He must try to take the curse off the whole story for her.

'It's no joke,' Liz said. 'Look, there are gannets diving.'

Far away in the distance the bright gleaming gannets were plummeting head first into the sea. They could just see the little splash and froth of white as each one entered the water.

'They go blind eventually,' said Liz and the pain in her voice wrung his heart. 'Diving in with their eyes wide open. And when they can't see to catch food they starve to death.'

'I know. I know.'

There were tears in her eyes and on her cheeks. He stretched out his hands to her but she ignored them, locked into her own misery, so he slipped his arms around her. Anything to comfort her. He could not bear her grief. She buried her head against the warmth of his body and stood like that for a long moment. He could feel her heart beating against him and he felt too an immeasurable tenderness for her, felt curiously responsible for her. Then she moved a little apart from him. 'It's cruel isn't it,' she said. 'But then the whole world's cruel.'

'Tell me what happened next.'

'Do you want to know?' She had turned away and her whisper was hard to catch. 'He drowned you see!' she said.

'Liz. Lizzie!'

She came and sat beside him and anchored her hand on his knee.

She was walking along a sandy beach fringed with turf and bent grasses and behind them a long low row of cottages. She was afraid. She could feel the fear welling up inside her. At high water mark there was a line of wreckage: broken spars and something else. Something she didn't wish to look at. A mess of weeds and feathers and shells. A bundle of old rags. She went closer, her legs dragging. She was dressed in wool. It was very uncomfortable: prickly and too warm with the sour stale smell of unwashed clothing. Perspiration broke out on her forehead. The bundle of old rags was very large. Much too large. She forced herself to look down and saw the drowned body of a young man lying face down in the sand, seaweed twined in his hair, flies rising from the corpse in a little angry cloud as she disturbed them. She saw sand falling in little runnels down the old leather oilskins that she knew had been his father's before him. 'Oh my dear God,' she said. Steve felt her tense against him.

'Who drowned?' His words shattered the picture into a thou-

73

sand fragments, but she knew, she remembered.

'The boy who had taken Marie to sea in the first place. He drowned. The boat was lost with all hands. The bodies were washed ashore later.'

'But they couldn't blame Marie Lamont for that could they?' Steve's rational New World voice broke in.

'Couldn't they? They'd seen her at the stone. With the other women. Nine of them. A coven. The stone was sacred remember? They'd seen her pushing it. She was different from the other girls. So they knew she was a witch. She wasn't like the others. They had to get rid of her. Don't you understand? They had to get rid of her.'

Danny had pulled the car into a layby. He drew a deep breath and tried to relax. Alice stared at him in anxiety.

'Are you not well?'

'I'm fine. I don't know what it is, but every time I start on about Elizabeth,' he paused. 'It's nonsense I know. But I just feel — nervous.'

'You must make her like you Danny.'

'But she's not natural. She's not interested in — well — normal things for a girl of her age.'

'What do you mean?' asked Alice defensively. 'Would you rather she had skin inches deep in make-up and spent all her spare time necking in corners like that friend of hers, Kate what's her name?'

'Kate's actually quite a nice girl when you get to know her.'

Alice grunted, non-committally. 'Well Liz is different.'

'You can say that again,' said Danny. He started the car again. 'Come on, let's go. We'll be late.' He drove off slowly and with unaccustomed care.

Liz and Steve sat in silence, the boat slopping gently about in the water. 'That's some story,' said Steve. He was at a loss for a more suitable comment so he stood up. 'We'd better get back in I think.' He didn't know what to make of any of it.

Help me, she thought. Help me please, or I'm lost. Aloud, she said, 'Do we have to? I could stay on the water for ever with you. Nothing matters out here.'

'You'd soon get cold and hungry and probably seasick too.' She did not respond. 'Come on,' he said. 'Enough witchcraft for one day. Ready to go about?' She sat still, staring back at the

74

town. 'Liz?' he said.

She smiled up at him. For the present she was safe. Clinging to the thought of him she was somehow less threatened by the engulfing past. But what will happen when he goes, whispered a treacherous voice in her head.

When Liz got home that afternoon Rose was waiting for her in the bedroom. The girl came marching in, full of her sailing, excited and supremely happy. Rose had never seen her so animated.

Damn Alice, she thought. She wondered just what her daughter saw in Danny and then admitted the unfairness of the thought. Alice was still a young woman. She had married young and conceived Liz immediately. She might even have more children, Danny's children. But what would Liz make of that?

'Why are you sitting in here gran?' asked Liz, surprised. It wasn't that she minded. Nothing was ever private from Rose. But it was unusual to find her grandmother sitting so quietly. She hugged the older woman.

'Oh gran it's been wonderful. You can't imagine.'

'I was just looking at your pictures and keeping your lizard company. Do you mind?'

'No. Why should I? You know you're always welcome in my room.' Liz went over to the glass tank and included the lizard in the conversation. 'I can't describe it,' she told him and then turned to Rose again. 'I can't describe how wonderful it was. Being on a boat. Being out there with Steve. Oh it felt so right gran. It's beyond words.'

'That's good. I'm glad you got your trip.' It was unlike Rose to be so preoccupied. Usually she shared her granddaughter's enthusiasms. And why did her voice sound so strangely flat? Something was wrong.

'What's the matter?' Liz demanded. 'You were waiting for me. Why?'

'I've got something to tell you.'

'What? Has there been an accident?' Liz visualised her mother, stretched out in hospital. Ill. Dead. Danny was an awful driver, she thought and then — Oh please let it be Danny. Not mum. Please let it be Danny.

'Oh no. Nothing like that.' Rose had forgotten her granddaughter's over-active imagination. Liz was capable of constructing a whole imaginary saga, tragic or otherwise, from a few words.

'What, then?' Liz clutched at Rose's arm with both hands, almost shaking her. 'What is it then?'

'It's about your mother and Danny.'

'What about them?'

'They've decided to get married.'

'Oh?'

A strange expression, something between amusement and malice crossed her face.

'Oh that.' She tapped the lizard's cage gently. He did not respond. 'So?' asked Liz.

'How do you feel about it?' asked Rose exasperated.

Liz turned a blank face toward her. It was, thought Rose, as though she had deliberately wiped it clean of all expression.

'Should I feel something about it?' A seemingly innocent question, full of guile.

'Yes of course you should,' Rose was stung into a quick response. 'Why are you behaving like this? I don't understand you these days. You're not like my Lizzie at all.'

'It won't happen. I know it won't happen.'

'What on earth do you mean?'

'It won't happen. I just know. So why should I waste my precious time worrying about it. Besides. I don't care what they do? It's nothing to do with me, is it?'

Liz was at the door.

'Yes. . . but. . .' Rose tried to detain her. 'Don't go Elizabeth. I want to talk to you.' But Liz was already out of the room. She went out of the flat, leaving the door wide open behind her. 'See you later.' Rose heard her call from the stair and then she was gone. She walked down towards the seashore deep in thought. Whatever happened, she must keep a brave uncaring face. But it wasn't easy. They all thought she was hard, Danny most of all. But there was a terrible pain that writhed and tore inside her, and threatened to break out in a storm of weeping. She had known exactly what was coming, had expected it for some time, and for all her assumed indifference had dreaded it. Now the marriage was a distinct probability. They must be serious or else they wouldn't have asked Rose to speak to her about it. She sat on the sea wall and stared out to sea for a long time. Danny and her mother. She thought about them together. Once, she had come home in the dusk and caught them kissing passionately, in Danny's car, leaning together uncomfortably with the gear stick between them. And once she had seen them walking along the main street of the town, holding hands, and a flush of intense embarrassment had burned her face. How could they do it, and in public too? Now they would be sleeping together and that was somehow the worst thought of all.

Last night she had lain awake and thought about Steve. She had thought about making love with him. It was not something that had preoccupied her much before, although her friends spent long hours over coffee and Coca Cola and illicit cigarettes, talking about boys, talking about sex, speculating, confessing, dissecting possible relationships. Once, when she was twelve, she had had a mad crush on one of the sixth year boys. She had shared her passion with Kate. It didn't matter that they both adored the same boy since neither of them had the remotest chance of doing more than admire the object of their affections at a respectful distance. But they had passed most of their spare time talking about him and watching him and had sent him an extraordinary valentine, more of a book than a card, full of romantic rhymes and pastel illustrations. Liz blushed hotly when she thought about it now. There had been no response from their blonde, blue eyed hero though no doubt he had laughed over it with his friends. He had left school soon after and gone away to university. Liz had seen him once in the long vacation a couple of years later and he had seemed shorter, heavier, spottier than the Viking of her memory.

After that, she had lost interest in the boys of her immediate circle, her affections reserved exclusively for her sailing heroes: Chay Blythe, Robin Knox Johnson, John Ridgeway. And although when Kate had recently confessed 'You know, almost all my thoughts are dirty!' she had laughed and pretended to agree, it wasn't true. Until she met Steve and sailed with him aboard the *Marie Lamont*, her mind had been too preoccupied with boats, and with her longing for the sea. And so it had been easy to shy away from physical or even emotional involvement. Besides, that was the way you got hurt. That was the way her mother had been hurt. Without making any conscious decisions she had nevertheless managed to suppress her own maturing emotions.

But she had a passionate nature and in Steve all that stifled desire found a sudden focus. The thought of his long, lean body aroused her into a frenzy of alien physical sensations. For the first time in her life she began to feel her own sexuality as a valid

77

part of her and not the faintly ridiculous weakness she had always scorned in others. The woman she would become welcomed the longing for this man, so attractive, so companionable, so gentle. But the unsubtle, inexperienced child retreated in terror from the enormity of such an attachment. It was much too frightening. She was not ready for such a rite of passage, for such an ordeal by fire. Meanwhile, her body, caught between the two, ached for him. She could not sleep. Sleeping, her dreams alarmed her. Waking, her fantasies appalled her. And when she thought of Danny and her mother she felt physically sick. Danny would be living in their house and sleeping in her mother's bed. How could she bear it? Her only consolation was that she was sixteen and needn't bear it, if only she could find somewhere else to go.

Once before, she had tried to run away. That had been when her parents were in the middle of their divorce, each so wrapped up in his or her own bitterness that nobody had really bothered to explain anything to the eight year old Elizabeth. She had blamed herself for the separation, cataloguing her small naughtinesses in her head, to try to account for it, wondering which of her crimes had finally driven her father away. 'Better if I go too,' she had thought and packed a little bag. It had all seemed so simple. She had put in a change of clothes and her nightie and a couple of favourite books: *Sea Stories for Boys* and *The Wind in the Willows*. Her teddy bear was too big to go in, so she had abandoned him, regretfully. Early one morning she had walked out of the house, running away like a girl in a story she thought. But then she had not known where to go. She had reached the end of the street and realised that the only place to which she was absolutely certain of the way, was her grandmother's house. So she had gone there, suitcase in hand, and rung the doorbell. 'I want to go to another land,' she told Rose. In stories people went into another land and lived happily ever after.

Now she no longer blamed herself for the divorce but nor did running away into another land seem such a simple affair as it had at the age of eight. 'Why Danny?' she thought for the hundredth time. Why couldn't her mother be content without a man? If the truth were told, and Liz wouldn't readily admit it, even to herself, she had liked Danny at first. When he had just been her teacher, they had got on very well. She was a clever girl and difficult though she might be, he had coaxed her to work for him at a subject she obviously disliked. It was only last year when Alice got the job as school secretary and when Liz gradually become aware that her maths teacher and her mother were becoming a little more than friends: it was only then that she had taken against him. She repeated to herself, 'Why on earth Danny?'

Tom found Liz sitting staring out to sea, as he walked home. Alone, thank God. He so seldom had her to himself nowadays.

'Hello,' he said. 'What're you doing?'

'Nothing much.'

Tom sat down beside her. 'I didn't expect to see you on your own. I thought you couldn't tear yourself away from Mr Freedom.'

'You don't have to stay you know. Nobody asked you to sit down, did they?'

'I'm sorry.' Why did he always have to say the wrong thing? 'What's the matter?'

'Nothing much.'

'Come for a walk.' He pulled her to her feet and retained her hand in his. It was icy cold. She followed him listlessly, allowing him to pull her along like a small child. They went down on to the beach. 'You'll get yourself talked about you know. Going on that boat with the American. He's old enough to be your father.'

'What will they do? Burn me for it?'

Tom didn't know what to make of the remark so he carried on walking in silence, giving her hand an occasional comforting squeeze.

A little ahead of them, lying face down among a patch of shiny brown seaweed was a drowned doll. It was an old doll, pink, bald and faintly sinister in the manner of all abandoned toys. Perhaps eighteen inches long, it lay there, its little arms raised above its head in supplication. Long thin strands of seaweed were twined around it. Tom was bending to pick it up when Liz pulled him back, her cold fingers digging into his arm, so sharply that her nails broke the skin.

'Ouch! What's the matter?'

'No,' she said. 'Don't touch it. Tom — leave it alone. Come away please.'

'Why?' he laughed. 'You've hurt my arm.'

'It's drowned.' Then she saw the figure lying face down among the seaweed. Face down on that other shore that was like this shore. The same and yet different. A young man. A young fisher lad. 'Oh my bonnie fisher lad.'

'It's only an old doll Lizzie.'

79

'Oh my bonnie fisher lad. Drowned.'

'Drowned?'

'Leave it be. Leave it be.'

She pulled him back up the beach, saying nothing until they came to a small children's playground with swings and a slide and a little merry go round. It was quite empty and they sat side by side on the swings, moving gently in syncopation.

'Just like old times,' said Tom, but when this failed to raise a smile, he asked 'What did you mean by drowned? It was only an old doll you know.'

Liz shrugged. 'It just looked drowned. Unlucky. Don't go on about it.'

'Do you remember when you fell off this swing and cracked you head open and you had to have stitches in it?

'I remember. I was eight. It was my birthday.

Her eighth birthday. Before the divorce. Before her safe little world fell apart. It was as if that injury, that bloody gash in her scalp, had split open more than her skin. Her father had been with her at the park as well as Tom and her mother had blamed him for the fall. 'You can't have been paying attention. You never do. I can't trust you.' She could still hear the angry words. Her head had been split open on the concrete and the blood had poured out. But her whole life had split open too, allowing pain and disintegration in.

'It was an awful day.' Tom spoke with real feeling. 'I thought you were dead.' Liz smiled at him. She remembered his ghost white face at the door, a few hours later when they had got back from the hospital. A doctor had stitched up the wound and, on learning that it was her birthday, had produced a Mars Bar from his top pocket, in the manner of a conjuror. Then Tom had come round. She had heard the doorbell and come to her bedroom door, to peep out. She was supposed to be resting but her head still throbbed with the pain. 'Please Mrs Finlay,' she heard Tom say. 'Is Lizzie dead?'

'All I was bothered about was whether or not they'd eaten the birthday cake in my absence. They hadn't of course. What a greedy little pig, I was!'

'Did you enjoy your sail?' asked Tom presently, seeing her more cheerful. She looked dreamily out to sea.

'Fine,' she said. 'Just fine. I'm getting good. Today the bay, tomorrow who knows?'

She stood up and moved away from the swing. Tom followed,

80

putting his arm around her shoulders. She didn't resist immediately but when he tried to kiss her she pulled back abruptly.

'Sorry,' said Tom.

'My fault. I'm not in the mood for it, that's all.'

Oh my bonnie fisher lad, drowned and dead. Dead and gone. Whose lament was filling her head? Whose sorrow?

Tom decided to try a different tack. 'I wouldn't mind going out on that boat myself. Do you think he'd take me out as well?'

Liz smiled a little secretive smile.

'I didn't think you were very keen on sailing.'

It was Tom's turn to take offence. 'Oh well, if you'd rather not have me with you.'

'Why on earth not?'

'I just thought. . .'

'Don't be silly. I don't fancy him or anything. He's much too old.' Lies, all lies. Tom looked sceptical. 'But he's good looking,' he said.

'How would you know what a girl would find good looking?'

'Well isn't he?'

'Maybe. But he's teaching me to sail Tom. That's what's important. That's all.' She took a perverse satisfaction in affirming this very partial truth. They had reached the sea wall again.

'My mum's going to be married.'

'To Danny?'

'What do you think?'

'Do you mind?'

'Of course I mind. I don't know why she wants to marry anyone again. Not after my father. Anyway — it'll never happen.' There was a pause. 'I'll never marry. Never.'

'You can't say that.'

'Oh yes I can. I know.' She turned to Tom with sudden warmth. 'Look I'll get Steve to take you out on the boat if you like.'

'You will? But will he want to take me?'

'He will if I ask him.' Tom wrinkled his nose, irritated by her self confidence. 'Oh aye,' he said and then quickly, before she changed her mind, 'I would like to come.'

He looked at his watch. 'I've to go home now. Coming?'

Liz stayed looking out to sea. 'No,' she said.

'You're sure you're all right now?'

'Sure.'

She waited until he was well out of sight, then walked back

along the seashore to where the doll lay. The tide was coming in and the water was lapping gently around it. She took a deep breath and, with a great effort, picked the doll up. It was heavy, heavy as lead, heavy as something drowned and dead. His oilskins soaked and heavy, his body heavy with water. Bloated. Turn him over. Turn him over, just to make sure.

She looked full at the doll and sighed with relief. Then she took it up to the sea wall where she left it high and dry, staring mutely out to sea, its arms stretched out to passers-by. Long before nightfall a passing small girl had carried it off in triumph.

Steve had tidied up the boat carefully, methodically, as always. He found the whole process of hosing down the deck, making sure that all was clean and secure, very soothing.

Afterwards, he cooked himself a meal. He had intended to relax and read but he found himself restlessly returning to the thought of Liz, to her inexplicable changes of mood, to the feelings of tenderness and protectiveness she aroused in him.

He put her resolutely out of his mind and went ashore, and drank too much in one of the bleak little seafront bars. In an upstairs lounge, a singer was bawling out 'Strangers in the Night' tunelessly, the amplification distorting the words into an anonymous blare of sound. Another solitary drinker, recognising him for an American, and remembering some ephemeral wartime friendship with a guy from Iowa bought him a pint of the beer the locals called 'heavy'. It was strong and warm and bitter. He returned the favour and then they sampled a variety of malt whiskies. Steve lost count of how many. Later, a fight broke out by the bar and fists and stools flew around his head but he sat on unperturbed. The fight subsided and the barman, admiring his cool, bought him another drink. He was simply too drunk to care. When he walked down the pontoon on his way back to the *Marie Lamont,* he trod with great care. He had, he realised, been trying to anaesthetise himself but he had not succeeded.

'Killing things. I hate it!' Her words still echoed around his head. He too had hated killing things. He remembered his first fishing trip with his father. How his heart had fluttered to feel the tug on his line and how proud he had been to land his first fish. His expectations of the excursion had been so high. But then he saw the little silvery creature flapping and struggling and gaping, out of its element, the sheen of its scales already dulled. 'What do I do now?' he asked his father in panic. 'Hit it over the head,' his father told him, laughing. But he couldn't do it. His father had to do it for him. Then Steve went into the bushes and was sick, dashing shameful tears from his eyes. A great lump of a boy crying over a fish. He was very much ashamed. He pretended that he had eaten a piece of pine resin. But he could not eat the fish.

And then when his father took him shooting that made him physically sick too. It was not that he was a coward. They could haul him up the tallest masts, to work there. He never flagged on sailing or walking trips, never turned down a dare, however foolhardy. No boy would challenge him to fight twice. He was cool, an undisputed leader of his pack and in his teens had acquired a reputation as something of a tearaway. For a long time he was heavily into bikes and studded leather, hard rock and tight blue jeans. His family despaired of him. Then he mellowed a little and found his niche in the world of sailing. But still, cruelty to helpless living things aroused a rage and horror in him that the boy had only been able to express through tears and physical sickness. As a man he controlled these reactions but the feelings were the same. Once, he caught two younger boys maltreating a cat, tying tin cans to its tail. He freed the terrified animal, getting badly scratched in the process and then turning on the tormentors, threatened them with such ominously controlled rage that they fled in terror from the murderous look in his eyes.

He saw Liz as a small helpless living thing subject to some great and nameless cruelty. He felt the same all consuming rage inside him but it was without focus. For once, he did not know what to do. He drank a very great deal of water, and fell asleep.

MARIE: 1662

One day, not long after Kettie had made me acquent wi' the devil I was at her house and feeling weary had fallen asleep in the box bed, at her bidding. Then the devil came in and kissed me where I lay. I was sorely tempted and I fell. I had been virtuous and had not known another man save Thomas and that only to kiss him. But the devil came to me naked in the night and entered into my body and took my maidenhead from me. My mither had tell't me to expect much pain at that time but it was not so, for he pleasured me greatly.

Then he bade me betake myself wholly to his service and said it would be well with me and bade me forsake my baptism which I did willingly, delivering myself to him and putting one hand on

83

the crown of my head and the other to the sole of my foot and giving all betwixt the two to him.

He gave me a new name: Clowts, because he said I was aye washing the clowts and pots and pans up at Ardgowan but he laughed most cruelly when he cried me by that name. And then he nipped me on the right side which was very painful for a time. But when I grat he took me in his arms to comfort me and he stroked my skin with his hand and healed it. And so I bear his mark to this day.

5

Early on Wednesday morning Rose was pouring her third mug of tea and one for Liz too. Alice was eating an unsugared grapefruit and pulling a face about it. She wore a smart pink jogging suit that was stretched too tight across her bottom. 'Nice sprinkling of brown sugar, that's what you need,' said Rose, who disapproved strongly of dieting. But then she had always been slender. Just as Alice looked at her watch, the doorbell rang. Danny was calling for her. He had persuaded her to go jogging with him though Alice had profound misgivings about the whole exercise. She went to open the door while Rose took Liz her morning tea.

Rose was quite unprepared for the empty bedroom, for the empty bed. Liz wasn't a particularly late riser but on holidays she was seldom up before Rose. The bed had been slept in, Rose noted with relief but the room was untidy with nightclothes still strewn about. Wherever Liz had gone, she had been in a hurry. Rose stood uncertainly in the doorway. Running through her mind was a memory of Liz's last attempt at running away, when she was eight, with the divorce impending. Another land, she thought. The lizard watched her curiously.

Alice was letting Danny into the flat. He too was dressed in a smart jogging suit and he was jiggling the change in his little zip-up pocket impatiently. 'We slept in,' said Alice apologetically.

'I thought you'd be ready.' Rose, just coming out of Liz's room, caught the little whine of indignation in his voice. It made her very angry, that time and again Alice pandered to it. Alice had done the same with her first husband and he had turned into a kind of petty tyrant, demanding and getting his own way at all times. 'She'll do it all over again,' thought Rose desperately and then, 'But Danny isn't like that, is he?'

'Liz isn't there,' she said.

'In the bathroom I expect.' Alice finished her tea with a gulp.

'Don't hurry,' said Danny, repenting of his impatience, as he always did. 'You'll be ill if you try to run with tea sloshing around inside you.' That was the good thing about Danny. Unlike Alice's first husband, his bad tempers were short lived and he never bore grudges.

'She isn't in the bathroom. I've looked.'

Alice panicked. 'Oh God,' she said, whirling about the kitchen. 'Danny, we'd better phone the police.' She moved towards the phone but Danny restrained her. Rose was glad of his presence.

'Hang on — hang on a minute. She could have gone out for a walk for all we know.'

Alice subsided into a chair. 'I suppose you're right.' She looked at Rose. 'Did you tell her anything — about — us. You know?'

Rose gave Alice Liz's untouched mug of tea. 'Here. Drink this. I told her something. Not much. She can't have run away though.'

'Why not?'

'She's left her lizard behind. And her piece of whalebone carving. She wouldn't go away and leave them just like that now, would she?'

'She would if she was upset. Besides, she couldn't take a lizard with her, could she?'

'No. But she'd ask somebody to look after it. And she'd take the carving. And leave a note. I'm positive.'

'But she was upset?'

'Well' — Rose glanced at Danny. 'Not really upset.'

'Then how was she?' demanded Danny.

'More disbelieving, I should say.'

Steve was tucked into a window seat on the Glasgow train, watching with avid interest as they crossed the River Clyde. The backyards of the city through which they had just travelled had been littered and decayed: grimy tenements, empty warehouses with shattered windows and abandoned council houses with doors like gaping mouths. But the skyline that he now saw — a mixture of Victorian and modern, at once so foreign and yet so familiar from photographs and descriptions — with the great river winding through the middle of it, silver grey in the morning light, gave him a lurching thrill of excitement. How had his great grandfather seen this place, he wondered?

In Central Station a steady stream of commuters poured off the trains and into the main concourse, Steve among them, admiring the vast Victorian splendours of the station. He had a moment of pure elation. Pigeons scattered before his feet. Sunlight filtered through the glass roof. He loved to travel by train but seldom found the opportunity at home.

Further back in the same crowd Liz pushed forward in an

effort to keep Steve in view but still uncertain as to whether she should let herself be seen. She was afraid of his anger, but afraid of losing him. She moved forward bravely as though to intercept him and then retreated. Don't be silly, she told herself. Surely he'll be pleased to see you. He likes you. He wouldn't have taken you out on his boat if he didn't like you.

All unawares Steve moved out of the station with Liz following cautiously behind. Suddenly she realised that he was about to get into a taxi: one of a long line of black cabs parked there in front of the station. Anxiously, she darted forward. 'Steve,' she said.

It was immediately plain to her that he was unpleasantly astonished to see her. Her heart sank. Hell, he thought, Henderson had been right after all. What was it the man had said? 'You'll never get rid of her now.' Striving to conceal his impatience he asked 'What are you doing here?' But when he saw the expression on her face; a sort of desperate reliance on him, his initial irritation melted. She was so transparent, so young and open that as usual, his heart went out to her.

He was angry. She could see that at a glance. Would he send her home? 'I thought I could show you round.' She faltered. The taxi driver moved impatiently in his seat. 'Can I take you somewhere, sir?'

Steve shook his head in exasperation at Liz. 'Look, we can't talk here. Better get in.' If she was just a few years older they might have made a day of it, he thought regretfully. He could have taken her round the city, bought her lunch, wined her and dined her and perhaps even taken her back to the boat and made love to her, easing the loneliness, stifling the ache. But she was only on the very threshhold of womanhood and he — he was thirty five, a little battered, a little cynical, but with too much of a conscience to do more than agree to look after her for a couple of hours. Would she agree to those terms, he wondered uneasily?

'The Mitchell Library,' he said to the taxi driver, as the cab pulled into the stream of traffic.

She had, he noticed, dressed up for the occasion. She was wearing a dress like a flame, bright red, so that it emphasised her black hair and — something he had not noticed before — the extraordinary pallor of her skin. Her eyes looked huge in the thin face, and there were dark circles around them. He realised suddenly that she looked ill and wondered why none of her family had noticed. It was a little like escorting a ghost around the city.

What the hell can I do about it, he thought. He felt the responsibility had been forced on him but there was no-one to blame but himself and he resented his own concern for her. The taxi crept from one set of traffic lights to another. 'Listen,' she said. 'If you don't want me I can go back home. I didn't mean to intrude.'

'You should have thought of that before you came all this way.'

'I thought you'd be pleased. I thought you liked me.'

'I do like you.'

Last night, she had ironed her dress. She had washed her hair and dried it, brushing it until it gleamed. This morning she had put on a little make-up and rather too much perfume. She had scarcely recognised the strangely adult face that stared back at her from the mirror. Did he even notice any of these things? Apparently not.

'I thought I could try to find out more about Marie Lamont at the Mitchell Library,' she told him. 'I do want to know more about her.'

Steve relaxed. 'You seem to know plenty already.'

At the Finlay flat Rose had just phoned Tom. Alice was lacing up her running shoes, with Danny hovering impatiently in the hall.

'Well?' she asked, as Rose put the phone down.

'Tom doesn't know where she is. Although she did mention something about going off for the day. He asked her out today and she said she couldn't go. She had other fish to fry. He thinks she might be with Steve Lamont.'

'I'll bet that's what it is,' said Danny. 'I told you not to trust him. They're all the same these bloody Yanks.'

'We don't know for sure where she is,' Rose spoke calmly.

'And I know she'll be safe enough if she's with Steve,' said Alice. 'I mean he looked very sensible to me.' She turned to Rose anxiously for support.

'Yes. I think you're right.'

'And she said nothing to you?' Alice asked her mother again.

'No. But don't worry.'

'It's not for the first time I'll bet. Come on love.' Danny opened the door. 'I expect she'll be OK.'

'She probably forgot to tell us or maybe she thought she had told us,' offered Rose.

'Or more likely thought we'd not let her go if she did tell us. Typical!' That was Danny again.

'She'll be back,' Rose forced herself to smile. 'Full of the joys. Don't worry now. Enjoy your jog.'

'Enjoy it?' Alice grimaced behind Danny's back but Danny was still full of righteous indignation about Liz and Steve. 'Typical!' he said.

Alice picked up her jacket and bag. They were driving to a nearby park so that they could jog with a modicum of anonymity and comfort. The park was very flat indeed. 'For goodness sake, will you stop saying that?' she told him sharply. 'Leave her alone. Stop criticising her all the time.'

'Well you do.'

'I'm allowed,' said Alice. 'I'm her mum.'

Danny knew when to keep silent. 'Let's go running,' he said.

Liz doubted if she would have dared to set foot inside the Mitchell Library, so imposing was the building, if it hadn't been for Steve. His casual confidence made everything seem easy. She envied it, and his air of friendly authority that made people willingly defer to him.

They sat opposite each other at one of the big reading room tables. Steve was looking through files of old newspapers bound together and making notes. Liz was reading, dipping into a small pile of old books. Steve, glancing across at her every now and then, saw only her bent head with a curtain of dark hair obscuring most of her face and most of what she was reading. But once he caught a glimpse of an old woodcut of a street fiddler, walking as he played, and once he saw a grotesque depiction of the burning of a witch on what seemed to be a horribly symmetrical bonfire, as though a great deal of trouble had been taken to get the pyre just right. For the most part though, Steve was completely engrossed in his old newspaper reports. When she was sure that he was not looking at her, Liz would watch him covertly. After a while though, he felt her gaze and glanced up at her, smiling. For Liz, it was as if the whole stuffy reading room had been suddenly and dazzlingly illuminated. He gave her confidence. With him, she could be happy and at peace with the world.

'I thought you were mad at me,' she whispered.

'I am,' he said, his grin belying the words.

'Find anything?' she asked.

'I think so. It's very interesting. Something here about my family.' He glanced at his watch. She was aware of him doing it; aware that his time was carefully apportioned and that she had only a very small part of it. The thought was painful to her, and she wondered what else she could do to make him notice her.

'Come on.' He stood up. 'I'll tell you all about it on the way. I've got to be moving or I'll be late. Give those books back and I'll meet you outside.'

They walked away from the library through the dusty city streets. It was a warm dry day and the roads were hazy with heat. Sparrows quarrelled on the pavements. Ahead of them a drunk searched a litter bin for cigarette ends. He glanced up at them as they passed, with sad hostile eyes but said nothing.

Danny and Alice were jogging around the seafront park, past the Crazy Golf, past the kiddies' playground where Liz had talked to Tom the night before. It was much too warm for jogging. Danny, who was fit, was enjoying it much more than Alice, who was not. She soon slowed down, almost to a walk. A little dog had been trotting after them, thinking it a big game and she bent to pat him. 'Wish I had four legs like you,' she told him.

Danny stopped and waited for her to catch up with him. 'How could she just go off like that and not tell us?' said Alice indignantly, remembering her daughter.

'I told you love. It's typical.'

They jogged on. Alice picked up speed but she was red in the face and hot, her chest heaving. The little dog got under her feet and almost tripped her up. He was summoned by his owner and bounced easily across the grass, tongue hanging out, mouth open in an engaging grin.

'You'll have to watch her with that American,' said Danny who seemed to be having no trouble in talking and running simultaneously though the phrases came out rather disjointedly.

'He's old enough to be her father!' said Alice, jerkily.

'So?'

Alice gave up the unequal struggle and slowed down again. 'Sometimes I think I hardly know her,' she said.

Danny had to wait for her once more. He was preparing to jog on when she collapsed on to a nearby bench, fanning herself desperately with her hands. 'God, I'm too old for this.'

'Who does know her?' said Danny, relenting and sitting down too. He closed his eyes for a moment. 'Stop her going on that boat,' he said.

Alice was horrified. She took a great gasp of air and steadied herself.

'Oh I couldn't do that.'

'Why not?'

'You don't understand. It's like a dream come true to her. She'd never forgive me if I stopped her sailing. Never.'

Liz and Steve had reached the walkway beside the Clyde. It was lunchtime and Liz could feel the beginnings of hunger. She had breakfasted early on a piece of bread and jam, too excited to eat much and afraid anyway of waking Rose, who was a light sleeper. On the train, she had visualised Steve asking her out to lunch. They would go to some smart restaurant she thought: elegant but casual. She would be able to talk about it afterwards to Tom and Kate.

'Steve and I had lunch together in Glasgow,' she would say and Kate would be green with envy. But she mustn't appear too eager and anyway, she badly wanted to know what Steve had found out in his old newspapers. As they walked along beside the river with the muted crash and roar of traffic as accompaniment she asked again, 'So what have you found?'

'My great grandfather was a fisherman,' he said. 'In your town. Well — it wasn't a very big town then. More a village I suppose.'

'I thought you said he had shares in a trading smack.'

'Yes, but before that he and his brother had a fishing boat. But the brother — it was his elder brother — Alexander Thomas Lamont — he was drowned.'

Something turned over inside her. There was a buzzing in her ears. Why were her fingers so cold? She clasped them together but they were ice against ice. I'm frightened, she thought. Help me. I'm frightened. Her heart fluttered, not with desire this time, but with panic. Her breathing felt constricted. Sickness washed over her. Thomas, fisherman of this parish. 'Drowned?' she asked.

'Yes. It was written up in one of those old newspapers back there. The boat sank and Alexander was drowned.'

A drowned man on the seashore, face down. Twined in shiny brown seaweed. Like the doll. But she had rescued the doll, hadn't she? Oh my bonnie fisher lad, what have I done? She slowed down and gazed at the river. Steve's voice went on: gentle, calm, interested. She clung to the voice, to the reality of the voice and the man, her anchor in the world.

'Robert — that was my great grandfather — he managed to get ashore. You know I figure he must have got involved with trading instead of fishing after his brother Alexander was drowned. The story goes that the poor guy was due to be married and his girl had been watching for the boat coming in.'

'And he never came?' Liz's voice was a whisper.

'Apparently not.'

'I wonder what became of her?'

Steve brushed the question aside. 'So what about Marie Lamont?' he asked. 'Did you find anything new?'

'She was brought here to Glasgow to stand trial. She came forward of her own free will. She came and offered herself willingly to trial saying that God had moved her because she had lived long in the devil's service.'

Was Liz quoting, he wondered and how did she remember it all so well? 'Poor girl,' he said aloud. There was something dreadful about such a confession. Such deliberate self destruction fascinated him. It was her belief in her own guilt that horrified him. What had persuaded her that she was a witch? What had been her state of mind? What had convinced a simple and presumably innocent country girl to make such a disastrous confession? Liz read his mind. 'She must have believed it, mustn't she? She must have thought that she really was a witch — mustn't she?' Steve reluctantly forced himself to turn away from her distress. He had a lunch date and he was already late for it. He hadn't asked her to come. 'Look,' he told her. 'I have to leave you here.' Moored on the river was an old boat, now used as a club and restaurant for ex Royal Navy officers. Liz looked from Steve to the boat in envious disbelief. 'Are you going aboard that?'

'I am. I've arranged to meet some old friends to talk about my schooner, my *Granny Kempock*. They might have some idea where she is. What will you do now? Go home?'

'No.' She was the sulky little girl again, all her plans crumbling. How can he do this to me, she thought. How can he just leave me here. He doesn't care about me at all.

'What will you do then?' He couldn't help being worried about her. He felt responsible for her but was unwilling to change his plans.

'Oh I'll be all right.' She spoke airily, defensively. I'll show him, she thought.

'Well I did warn you not to come honey. I told you I had things to do.'

'Yes, I know. I'm too young and I'm a girl. I know.'

He spoke firmly but not unpleasantly, deliberately cool.

92

'That's just about the long and short of it honey. You are too young.'

'I'm not.'

'You're much too young. You know that Liz.' He felt like a prize monster.

'I'll wait for you,' she said. It was one last try. He could see that she was very near to tears. 'I don't know how long I'll be,' he told her. 'I'm deserting her,' he thought and then, 'but what else can I do?'

'No,' he said. 'You'd better go home now. Take care.'

Before he could change his mind he forced himself to turn and walk away from her. He could feel her eyes on his back, full of longing and acute misery. For a few seconds he hated himself and her, for rousing impossible emotions in him. Then he pulled himself together, consciously. She watched him board the boat, all her wonderful and carefully constructed daydreams shattered.

All the way up on the train that morning she had imagined them having lunch together. She had assembled conversations in her head: his questions and her replies. She would tell him all about herself, Liz Finlay, her own hopes and fears. They wouldn't talk about Marie Lamont at all. She had imagined herself with a wit and intelligence beyond her years. 'Why not come and crew for me?' he would say. 'I'm sick of sailing alone and you're a natural. A real natural. I've never met anyone who's taken to sailing like you.' She could almost hear the admiration in his voice. 'I've never met anyone quite like you Lizzie.'

But now none of this had happened. Nothing ever happened the way you wanted it to, the way you imagined. The other person always did or said the wrong thing. She walked away dejectedly. The feeling of utter rejection was like a great hard knot in her chest, a real physical pain that twisted and turned in there and threatened to squeeze the humiliating tears out of her eyes. She never cried, never. She sat down on a bench beside the river. A drunk old man clutching a whisky bottle swerved towards her. She was very frightened. She got up and walked quickly away, glancing behind her to make sure that he was not following. But he had sat down on the bench and was drinking greedily from his bottle. Steve's right, she thought. I'm too young. I shouldn't be here. In the distance she could hear fiddle music and that meant people. Surely if there was a busker there would also be people listening. She walked as quickly as she could towards the high rhythmic sound.

93

In the smart bar aboard the boat a small group of men were standing with pints of lager. One of them, a marine historian of some distinction was also an old friend of Steve's. He and Steve had corresponded about their mutual interest in maritime history, for years. James wrote books about old sailing ships in his spare time. He was a florid, middle aged man with a carefully brushed moustache, long hair deliberately plastered across his bald head and the beginnings of a paunch. 'I've always thought I'd like to cross the pond,' he said to Steve, when Steve had been supplied with his own cool glass. 'But never on my own.'

'Well you do get a bit sick of your own company,' Steve admitted. 'So how's the latest masterpiece going?'

'The book's going pretty well you know but I don't get enough time. There's never enough time.'

'And what about my *Granny Kempock*? Did you come across anything about her?'

'Well,' said James conspiratorially, 'I might just have come up with some information for you there.'

With the air of a conjuror he brought out a faded photograph of an old topsail schooner. Steve looked at it closely. 'Yes. I believe that's her.' He seemed disappointed. 'Your picture's older than the one I've got though.'

James leaned forward. 'Ah but I can tell you when and where that was taken. Some time in the forties she'd been on her way to Northern Ireland. She foundered but didn't sink. She was towed into port — that's Port Glasgow there in the background. And there she sat for years, mouldering away.'

'Jeez,' said Steve with feeling. 'I wish I'd been around then.'

'Well in the late fifties a German businessman bought her and had her renovated on the Clyde and refitted as his own yacht.'

'I see.'

'Your picture must have been taken then.'

'But where did she go after that?'

'Ah well. To Italy I think.'

'That's a hell of a big place to explore. Lots of coastline,' said Steve reflectively. 'But thanks anyway.'

'I hope you find her,' said James. 'There's a painting of the old *Granny Kempock* in the art gallery up at the university. Big canvas. Squally weather, or some such title. Lots of ships, you know.'

'Is there?' Steve was surprised. 'I'll go and see her. Let's have another round before lunch,' said Steve, fishing out his wallet.

Liz was following the sound of the fiddle across a road and down a little alleyway between buildings. The alley ended in a court-yard at the back of a pub. This was old Glasgow and oddly unchanged by the years. The sun filtered down into it and warmed the old stones. The courtyard smelled strongly of tobacco though glancing around Liz could see nobody smoking. A young man was standing in the middle of a small group of bystanders, playing the fiddle. He was thin, bearded and intense. He stared straight at Liz, his eyes bright blue, piercing, uncanny. The notes of the violin wailed about Liz's ears, spiralling into her head, conjuring up strange images of dancing. Children and office workers, out for lunch were listening entranced by the young man's music. An old woman fed pigeons from a bag of stale bread. The birds fluttered down into the courtyard from their roosts on high ledges, momentarily obscuring the sunlight as they swooped and flapped and pecked in an intricate dance. The children were jigging up and down in time to the music. Liz felt eerily nostalgic as though this scene were something she had participated in before. The young man was playing to and for her alone. The notes grew faster and wilder, soaring higher and higher, making her dizzy, dazzling her eyes. Her feet itched to dance. It was as though the notes had crystallised in her head and were suspended shimmering there, like icicles. But why was the fiddler wearing such strange clothes, like an old picture; and then she herself, the familiar twentieth century Liz was growing remote and distant and it was entirely natural for her to be stand-ing there watching this man in his dark tunic and homespun woollen trousers.

A group of women were dancing around him in a ring, hands joined. Dancing in their shifts of white linen, dancing without care, flinging sturdy bodies from side to side, laughing and aban-doned to the music. But still the young man looked at her, sum-moning her to dance. The notes reached a crescendo and now she could feel them pulsing in her bones, as though her very sinews were vibrating in time with the strings.

'Dance,' he said and the women caught up the chant.

'Dance, dance, dance with us.' She could not withstand them. She joined the circle. She was in the ring and part of it. 'Never come back again,' she said. 'Go away to a strange land and never come back again.'

She heard one high sweet note on the very brink of existence and surely she would disintegrate totally, be at one with the dance itself. It was what she most desired. But Liz, Elizabeth, was afraid. She held back, terrified of losing herself, and still the music, strong and sensuous, enticed her. With a tremendous effort she broke away and ran from the circle. Behind her she could hear the busker laughing. The pigeons scattered in alarm as she fled.

Steve was walking along the riverbank when Liz came careering around a bend in the path as if, he said later, all the devils in hell were after her. Unseeing, she ran straight into his arms, so forcefully that she almost winded him. She stared up at him with terrified eyes. 'No,' she said emphatically, though not to him, she was sure. She was looking out and beyond him, seeing nothing that he could see. But her panic was composed of exhilaration as well as fear. He held her and shook her gently. 'Hey,' he said. 'Hey Liz. It's me you know.'

'We met with the devil,' she said wildly. Was she laughing, or were there tears in her eyes?

'What are you talking about?'

'We met the devil and he sang and played to us and we danced. Oh we danced! We danced until we dropped.' She looked up at him and now he saw that she was laughing.

'He held me. I was part of him. Oh maister! Hold me in your arms aince mair! I've waited so long for you. Oh please hold me again.'

'Lizzie!' he said again. 'It's me. Steve. Remember me?' She faltered and looked up, directly at him. 'Steve?' The name came out wonderingly. She was herself again. That was always the way it was, as though someone had switched on a light behind her eyes, or perhaps switched it off. A distinct change would cross her rather beautiful face and she would become a different girl. For all her youth she could seem beautiful he thought, though never pretty. It was a dark, uncanny, uncommon face. She collapsed against him, sobbing. He took her to a bench where he put his arms around her and babied her, patting her back, stroking her hair. It seemed to be what she needed. But he was perplexed. Was she playing games with him? Telling stories as Henderson had warned him? She drew away from him and smiled up at him, half heartedly, her shoulders still shaken by the occasional sob. 'I'm sorry, I panicked a bit.'

'Do you often dance with the devil?' he enquired.

'What?' She sounded shocked by the question.

'Oh never mind. Just something you said.'

'There was a man playing the fiddle. Here he comes. Look.'

A young man came round the corner. He wore jeans and a tee shirt that said, 'Save the Whale.' A small dog trotted after him. He looked at Liz and grinned in a friendly fashion without threat or malice.

'So,' said Steve. 'He looks harmless enough.'

'I'm afraid of him.'

'Why? What did he do?'

'Nothing. He just played. I don't know why I was afraid. Something to do with the place itself. Where he was playing. A little courtyard. The sunshine and the pigeons and the sound of the fiddle. The notes were trapped among the buildings. I don't know why I was so scared.'

'Come on,' said Steve. 'You might as well come with me now. I'm going up to the University Art Gallery. There's a picture I want to see.'

She got unsteadily to her feet.

'Here,' he said. 'Take my arm.'

She slipped her arm through his. She felt his warmth flow into her, comforting her. It was not what she had planned but it was a start.

Rose sat by the Kempock Stone looking down towards the sea. She had been to visit her flat again and had as good as agreed to take it. But as she flicked through the brochure she was distracted, as though she could feel the intensity of her granddaughter's experience, as though she were somehow in tune with it.

Steve and Liz walked through the city centre. 'We can go by underground,' said Liz. 'It's quicker.' She was embarrassed to think of her recent behaviour. Trying to distract him and herself she stopped to look at a shop window full of tartan tammies.

'You must have one of those,' she told him.

'Why?'

'All Americans buy tartan tammies.'

'Do they?' He was amused. 'Well not this American.' He looked at his watch again. It was a habit with him. He always thought he might have kicked it when he was at sea, when the sun meant more to him than any clock. But as soon as he set foot on land again he tended to check out his watch all the time, trying to fit as much into his days as possible. 'Come on,' he said. 'Let's get going.'

On the small orange train they were forced to sit very close together, their knees touching. 'This is the clockwork orange,' she told him. 'I don't much like it.' She sniffed at the familiar earthy scent of the underground. It reminded her of newly dug potatoes, or the coal cellar at her grandmother's old house.

'Why don't you like it?' he asked. 'Claustrophobia?'

'I suppose so. I'm always afraid of getting stuck in a powercut or something.'

'Your imagination is much too vivid for your own good.'

'I know.'

'Sufficient unto the day, that's my motto.'

'What?'

'Sufficient unto the day is the evil thereof. Don't you know your bible?'

'Oh. Yes. I see.'

He patted her knee and laughed. 'Never mind kid. Never mind.'

In the art gallery it proved very difficult to identify the painting which depicted the *Granny Kempock*. There was a large nineteenth century canvas called 'A squall off the lighthouse' which showed a melée of sailing boats in bad weather. Steve peered closely at it. 'I can't make out the names of the vessels, can you?'

'No.' Liz stood beside him, looking at the picture. She had gone very quiet. Steve talked on, unaware of the change in her.

'I suppose it could be that one.' He pointed to a schooner in the thick of it, riding out the storm under bare poles.

'Oh no. That one's much older. Much older.' Liz was unable to take her eyes off the picture. But she saw no schooner, only a very old clinker built fishing boat and it was sinking. Why was he showing her this? How could he be so cruel?'

At the Kempock Stone Rose stood up, reached through the railings and touched the cold gritty surface, frowning slightly.

In her mind, Liz too stood by the Kempock Stone but it was unfamiliar, set up on a bleak hillside amid rock and heather. Where were the houses and streets of the town? A well trodden path led down the hill away from the stone. There were others with her. She saw them and recognized them: Kettie Scott, Margaret Holm, Jean King. Their names came into her head. She was with them and of them. They were her friends.

The wind was blowing in strongly from the sea, shepherding

big grey skeins of cloud before it. The rain lashed her, soaking her woollen skirt through to the heavy linen petticoat. She was aware of a row of long low cottages encircling a little harbour. A reek of smoke hung over the village. 'You're all alone in the world now Marie Lamont. But you have us. We'll not desert you. You have us.' Which of the women had spoken? She opened her eyes and looked at the picture again.

She was aboard a boat. It was a small open boat but the same women were there. Sea and sky were moving. She tried to fix her eyes on the horizon but that was pitching and tossing too. There was no fixed point. Her whole world felt as if it were dissolving around her, her mind completely disorientated. She felt her head and her stomach turn. She was cold and sick, cold and sick. She had never been so seasick before. Not when she was out with Tom. Even Kettie's remedy did not help her. The wind wailed about her head, about the hilltop like the notes of a crazy fiddle. And where was the boat? Where was she? Where was Liz Finlay?

'It was sic a storm,' she said. 'Sic a storm as they should never have been out in. Sic a storm as I have never seen.'

'What storm?' asked Steve. She was standing on the beach. The storm raged about her. Sand blew into her face and her lips tasted of salt. In the sand, a doll was lying face down with damp seaweed twisted about it. She moved towards it, struggling to get closer but her limbs were heavy and would not obey her. No. It was not a doll at all. It was the body of a man, wearing old fashioned leather oilskins. With an effort of will she forced her legs to carry her forward. She moved towards it, stretching out her hand, but still she could not reach the man. It was too difficult and besides, she didn't want to reach him, terrified of what she might find.

'Oh no,' she said. 'No. I would have saved you if I could. I would have saved you my dear. Oh I never meant for you to drown.'

'Liz!' Steve was shaking her by the shoulder. She stared at him blankly for a moment. He saw the colour leave her face. She cried out and then fainted dead away, crumpling at his feet. That at any rate was no pretence.

By the stone Rose shivered, staggered and almost fell. 'Oh Lizzie, Lizzie,' she said. She had to cling to the railings until the dizzy spell passed.

Liz saw blurred anxious faces hovering above her. She heard a babble of voices, far away at first and then coming gradually like her vision into focus. Steve and a gallery attendant were leaning over her. Steve was holding her hand in both of his. She felt his cool dry fingers on hers.

He saw her eyes open and, helped by the attendant, managed to get her into a chair. 'Thank you. I think she'll be all right now.'

'I'm sorry.' She clutched at Steve's hand again and held on tight. 'Did I faint? I'm so sorry.'

'You haven't had anything to eat, have you?' said Steve, guiltily, blaming himself. She shook her head. I keep forgetting that she's just a kid, he thought. Or perhaps I remember it too much. Perhaps I should just do what comes naturally and stop agonising over it.

'Will I get you a taxi sir?' asked the attendant, handing over a glass of water.

'Liz? What do you want to do?'

She drank, trying to pull herself together. She felt very cold. Her teeth chattered against the glass.

'No. I'm all right now. I'd just like some fresh air. I'll be fine. Honestly.'

What a thing to do, she thought and in public too. Steve saw colour returning to her cheeks, with relief. 'Take it easy then.' He put his arm around her and helped her to her feet again. Her legs seemed to have no strength in them at all. They walked slowly to the Botanical Gardens nearby and sat on a bench in the shade of a big horse chestnut tree. Liz was weepy and disinclined to talk. Besides, what could she say to him that would not sound as if she needed a psychiatrist. 'I have visions. Moments when I think I might be somebody else.' How could she say that aloud? How crazy it would sound.

'Have you told the doctor about all this?' he asked and when there was no response continued, 'Because you should. You don't look at all well to me.'

'I haven't told anyone. How could I? I don't need a doctor. I don't know what I need. But how could I tell anyone and what is there to tell? It all sounds — incredible.'

'How long have you been feeling like this?'

'Like what? I don't know how I feel. That's the problem. I don't understand what's happening to me.'

'Did you see something in the picture that frightened you?' he asked.

She got up. 'Let's walk,' she said. He followed her inside one of the big Victorian glasshouses. It was another world in here, a moist, warm, scented place. Climbing plants festooned themselves around the walls. A cactus reared up like a prickly green monolith. Liz relaxed a little. 'It's as if I don't want to understand,' she said. The warmth and strangeness of the place had soothed her. It was easier to talk. Easier to try to explain. 'I have all these pictures in my head but I don't want to understand them. When I was little I used to have nightmares. I had one dream that came back again and again. I was trying to close a door against — I don't know what. Something that frightened me. Something terrible.'

Steve nodded. 'I know those dreams. I used to have them too. But you grow out of them.'

'First the lock broke and then the handle and then the hinges and I was left trying to hold the door but it crumbled in my hands. And that's what it's like. Trying not to know, not to let it in. Not to understand. Because if I do. . . .' Her voice trailed away.

'What?' asked Steve.

But she wouldn't answer. She walked out of the glasshouse and sat down on the grass, picked a daisy that had somehow escaped the mower and began to tear off its petals. Steve sat beside her. He had bought a couple of sandwiches at a little shop on the way into the park and now he handed her a packet. 'Come on,' he said. 'Eat up. It'll make you feel better.' She took the sandwich and then put it down on the grass, too preoccupied to eat.

'I saw an old boat in that picture. An old fishing boat. And somebody lying on the beach. Somebody drowned.'

'There was nobody in that picture Lizzie. Just ships. Just boats. Nobody drowned.'

'No. I know that. I know that in my head.' If only he would understand. She tapped her breast. 'It's in here. In my heart. That's what counts. Oh God Steve . . . what's the matter with me?' She laughed suddenly. 'Me? Who am I talking about when I say me? I don't even know that any more. I don't know who I am.'

'Try and relax.'

She lay back on the grass and closed her eyes, one arm flung over her face to shield her eyes from the sun.

'Rest now,' he said. 'We'll go home when you're feeling better.' Steve sat up on one elbow watching her. Presently he saw her arm move down. Her body went rigid and then relaxed in an atti-

tude of sensuous abandon, arms flung backwards on either side
of her head, one knee bent, her face turned just a little towards
him. Why did he feel that something had changed, something
was different?

'We met with the devil and he sang and played to us and we
danced.' She spoke quite low with her eyes closed but the words
chilled him. Then her eyes flickered open. Was she seeing him,
he wondered and if not, what was she looking at? Steady on, he
thought, don't let it get to you too. You'll soon be as mad as she is.

'Marie Lamont,' he said. 'That's what *she* did Liz, not you.
You only read that in an old book.'

'No. You don't understand. It's always happening. Over and
over again. She wants to go to sea.' Her voice wavered. She sat
and caught at his hands. 'They won't let me. He drowns.' Her
breath caught in a sob.

'But that's just an old story.'

She brushed his words aside. 'And then I lay with that man.'

'What man Liz? What man?'

'In the box bed. I thought I loved him. I thought he loved me.
There was no-one left to love me. I wanted to be close in his arms
and to be loved and so I lay with him when he came to me. Kettie
said 'twas right and I believed her. And it was good, oh so good.
Oh you don't know! But then later, he wasn't kind to me. Oh no,
he wasn't kind to me. He left me. I thought he might come back
when I had need of him. I thought maybe he might save me. But
he never came.'

'What are you talking about Lizzie?'

'You see I gave all betwixt these two to him.' In a curious
gesture that sent a shiver down his spine she put one hand to her
head and the other to her heel.

'To who?'

'I did deliver myself wholly to him.' The voice was strong now,
the accent very broad. It was not like Liz's voice at all. 'I put this
hand to my head and this to my foot and I gave all betwixt the two
to him. It was wrong of me. It was very wrong. It was a great sin.
Who will ever forgive me now? Dear God I cannot even forgive
myself.'

'But who are you talking about?'

'Why, the devil of course!' she said.

MARIE: 1662

It was at about this time that my father was killed by falling into the burn when he was on his way home from Allan Orr's ale-house. He was drowned and I blamed Allan's wife very much for sending him home when she knew the weather to be so bad and he in no fit condition. And I thought it terrible, he a fisherman all his life and to be drowned in a burn. Also Allan Orr had the house where Margret Rankine was tenant and he had put her out in favour of his son and she threatened him that he and his wife would not be long together.

Soon after I was at a meeting with Jean King and Kettie Scott and Margret Rankine and the devil was there in the shape of a big brown dog that came with Kettie. Then myself and Kettie Scott, we came to Allan Orr's house in the likeness of cats and followed his wife into the chamber where we took a herring out of a barrel and having taken a bite left it behind us. Allan's wife must have ate the herring for soon after, she took heavy disease and died, so she did.

Then me and Kettie Scott and Margret Rankine and several others went out to sea betwixt Gourock and the lands of Arran, to do skaith to boats and ships and to raise stormy weather to hinder boats frae killing the fish. We caused the storm to increase greatly and meeting with Colin Campbell's ship did rive the sails from her and we met with my Thomas but I would not have him harmed, though he would not even look at me.

This was the first time that I had been at sea since two years before with Thomas. I was so overset with the ill weather that I took the fever and was very ill for many days after.

Kettie Scott tended to me at her house and as I lay in the box bed I dreamed that the devil did come and lie with me and fondle my naked body and did take me to him many times.

This happened during many nights and I repent me of it that I took sic a great pleasure in wrong doing, for it was a very great sin.

6

It was Thursday before the repercussions from Liz's trip to Glasgow began to reverberate through the Finlay home. On Wednesday night Alice had been far too relieved at the sight of her daughter to be angry. Rose refused to get involved, beyond saying mildly that she ought to tell her mother where she was going in future. But the following morning over breakfast, Liz was taken to task by her mother and grandmother. She feigned complete innocence.

'What was so wrong about me going to Glasgow?' she asked plaintively, over tea and toast. 'I'm sixteen. Not a child.'

'There was nothing wrong with you going. Just that you didn't tell anyone,' said Rose. 'Your mum was very worried.'

'Well it's the first time she ever has been worried,' said Liz defiantly, not looking at Alice.

'You know that's not true,' Alice defended herself hotly.

Liz had the grace to look ashamed.

'Were you on your own?' her mother continued.

'No. I went with Mr Lamont. With Steve.' A look passed between Alice and Rose but Liz intercepted it. 'I went to help him at the library. And I'm going on his boat today. But it's all right. Tom's coming too, so you needn't worry about me.'

'But we do worry about you love,' said Alice helplessly. 'We never knew he'd asked you to go to Glasgow.'

'He didn't really. I just went.'

'Oh Lizzie!'

'And then he thought I'd asked you if I could go. That you'd said it was all right.'

'So you lied to him.'

'Only a bit. And it wasn't his fault was it?'

'I'm sure it wasn't but that doesn't make it any better.'

'I can go sailing today, can't I?'

When Danny was absent Alice felt much more confident about making her own decisions. 'Yes. I suppose you can,' she said. 'So long as Tom's going too.'

It was a fine calm day on the Clyde with little patches of breeze ruffling the surface of the water and high clouds dappling the far hills with moving shadows. Steve helped by Liz and Tom, had sailed the *Marie Lamont* up the Holy Loch. Tom had begged a day off work and his father who had rather taken to the American had readily acquiesced. The boy had been delighted, both at the prospect of a day with Liz and at a day spent on Steve's boat. Although he never would have admitted as much to Liz, he secretly rather admired Steve.

For Liz, however, the trip was proving to be a disappointment. It was apparent that the addition of Tom to the party had subtly altered the relationship between herself and Steve. Perhaps her anticipation of it all happening in precisely this way had somehow affected her behaviour so that now, in many small ways, she found herself beginning to take second place to Tom. Perhaps she brought it on herself. Certainly Steve had no very clear intention of excluding her, though he had decided to try to distance himself a little from her. He felt, not without regret, that he could only help her by being sane and solid and normal and by staying remote from her.

If I get too involved with her problems I'll only add to them, he thought. And so he quite deliberately paid more attention to Tom. Besides, the Freedom was complicated for a beginner and there were many things which Tom must be taught, in a rudimentary fashion. Liz had got the hang of everything very quickly. Tom was slower and more methodical but Steve liked his dry sense of humour, and enjoyed the boy's company. He was much less demanding than Liz and more relaxing and so Steve left Liz to her own devices for a time. She mooched about the boat feeling restless and excluded.

'Take the helm,' said Steve to Tom as he had to Liz. 'Try to get the feel of it. Feel what the wind's doing . . . what will be best for the boat.'

Tom stood proudly at the wheel, the wind ruffling his hair. He felt like an advertisement for something. Something tough and macho: cigarettes, or alcohol or even, he thought with a grin, aftershave. None of which he indulged in to any great extent. 'This is great,' he said and Liz knew that for Tom, this was an admission of enormous happiness.

'I think we've got him hooked Lizzie,' said Steve but Liz only stared morosely at the sea. Jealousy stirred mutinously inside her.

Steve was amused by Liz's sulks but he wouldn't let her get away with them. 'Make us some coffee eh?' he said.

'But I want a go at helming.'

'Look,' said Tom with heavy humour. 'Do as the man tells you. There's a good girl, eh? Get down to the galley where you belong!'

'Oh you shut up.' Liz turned on Tom violently but Steve intervened. 'You don't have to be a good girl. And I don't expect you to be a galley slave. You know that. But I want coffee, he's helming and I'm watching him. So just get that kettle on and then you can take over. Have your turn.'

Liz went below. She put the kettle on the little stove, lit the gas and sat on a bunk waiting for it to boil. She felt miserably neglected. 'I hate them,' she thought, childishly and stared at herself in Steve's mirror. 'I'm pretty,' she thought, 'so why doesn't he notice?' She was immediately ashamed of herself. What did it matter what she looked like and why should he care? He was a man and she felt like a child. He thought she was too young. Why else would he call her 'kid' all the time. She *was* too young. She felt gauche and silly and afraid of her own emotions. Afraid of him. Sometimes when he frowned at her in exasperation she felt a little thrill and shiver of fear, but it was sensual too that fear. It excited her. And she could neither understand nor cope with it. She had wished for a boat as Marie had wished for a boat and here she was, sailing. So why was she not content? What more could she want? I'm a better sailor than Tom, she thought, so why do I feel so left out, such a misfit today?

Who looked back at her from the mirror? Herself or somebody different? Was that her own face, or not? I'm a wicked girl, she thought. Wicked, to have such thoughts. Wicked to dream such dreams.

'We're coming up to the American base,' said Tom, warningly, on deck. 'They send a patrol boat out to see you off if you get too close.'

'We'll go about then,' said Steve. 'Get ready.'

As the boat swung and heeled over Liz was flung backwards onto Steve's bunk. Disorientated, she covered her face with her hands. Steve poked his head down through the hatch.

'Are you OK Liz?'

'I'm a bit sick.'

'Come up then. You'll be better up here on deck. Tom can make that coffee.'

'No.' The kettle was boiling. 'I'll finish it now.'

In a few moments she was up on deck, bringing coffee in

Steve's bright plastic mugs.

'Come and take the wheel,' Steve said. 'It'll make you feel better. Come on Tom. Liz's turn now.'

Tom was reluctant to move. 'I'm enjoying myself,' he said. 'She's been out before.'

'Come on.' Steve was firm. 'Let her take over now.'

Liz took the wheel. She was better at this than Tom and she knew it. She had an instinctive feel for it.

'Look straight ahead at the horizon,' said Steve. 'There now.' He stood behind her for a moment, placing his hands over hers, setting her right. 'Better?'

'Fine. I'm fine now. Thank you!'

Tom was watching them. He too was very jealous. He saw Steve's brown hands covering Liz's small fingers and hated the gesture. 'You haven't felt seasick before have you?' asked Steve.

'It must be me,' said Tom.

'It is,' said Liz succinctly.

'Oh leave the poor guy alone can't you?' Steve moved away from Liz. 'Don't you ever stop bickering you two? Give me a break or I swear I'll put you both ashore. Either that or I'll have you walk the plank.' Tom and Liz looked guiltily at each other. 'I like a little peace on board so give a guy a break will you? OK?'

'OK,' they said. 'Just for now,' implied Liz's rather grim expression.

Alice and Rose were sitting outside a little block of sheltered flats in a small garden that was both vivid and fragrant with summer flowers. They looked back towards the building.

'Liz needs you, you know,' said Alice. She knew it was much too late for arguments. Rose had made up her mind. She could be quite as stubborn as her grand-daughter when it suited her. 'I just think it would be better if you stayed on with us. I mean nothing's final yet, is it?'

'It is as far as I'm concerned.' Rose was gentle but firm. 'It's not far away. Liz can visit me whenever she likes. She might be glad to get away.' She halted. That had been tactless, she thought, wishing that she could call the words back. But Alice pounced on the implication. 'You mean she might be glad to get away from Danny?'

Rose sighed. 'No — no but you two won't want me there all the time. And you might be glad of the occasional break from Lizzie too. Well Danny will. Be honest.'

107

'But I don't want you to feel that we're driving you out.'

Alice had always been too attached to her mother. Rose knew it and perhaps she had encouraged it. They had been three women living harmoniously together. A perfect threesome, until Danny came along. Why did men cause such chaos? Sometimes she felt resentful. Why couldn't Alice have just let things stay the way they were? But that was very selfish. I'm just a selfish old woman, she thought. It's better this way. Alice was still young and she needed a man, needed a lover. When Danny was around Rose occasionally saw her blossom into happiness, saw her arouse a kind of tenderness in Danny that was all the more startling for being unsuspected. Who was she to deny them the contentment they might achieve together?

'Look,' she said. 'I know what Liz feels like. In some ways growing old is rather like growing up again. I know how she feels. I need some more independence too.'

'You?'

'Yes. Can you not see that Alice?'

'I never thought of it.'

'Then you should. Because it's true.'

They left the garden and Rose took Alice out to lunch in a busy self service cafeteria nearby. Alice was pushing the remains of a tired salad about her plate. 'What will Liz do if you move out?' she asked.

Rose scraped up a lemon sponge pudding with relish. 'Oh, she'll get used to it. She wants her freedom too you know. She'll understand, I'm sure.'

'Danny's not happy you know. He thinks she ought not to see that American any more. Specially not after the Glasgow excursion.'

'She came to no harm. More coffee?'

'No thank you. And you've had enough too, mother. It isn't good for you.'

'Don't nag me Alice.'

'I care about you.'

'I know but I can take care of myself. I am old enough you know.'

'Danny's right in a way. Steve Lamont is much too old for her.'

'I think that she's much more interested in the boat than the man. She's got a crush on the boat if you like.'

'Yes but what about him?'

'What do you mean?'

Alice leaned closer. 'Well, you know. I mean she's a pretty girl.'

'You can trust him, I'm sure.'

'But she looks so much older than sixteen when she's all dressed up.'

'He knows she's only young. Stop trying to cast him as the villain. That's Danny talking, not you. You know he's all right. He's that old fashioned thing, an honourable man.'

Alice smiled, 'I suppose he is.'

A pair of women came up with trays looking for a vacant table. 'Excuse me, are these seats taken?' one of them asked.

'No. No.' Alice moved her bag rather grudgingly. The two women made themselves comfortable with large plates of fish and chips before them.

'But all the same she shouldn't be going around with an older man. Not at her age. Not alone,' said Alice firmly. 'It'll get her a reputation.'

The women glanced at each other, eyebrows slightly raised.

'You mean she should have a chaperone,' suggested Rose, laughing. 'Who do you think? Me or Danny?'

Alice lowered her voice. The women tried to listen without appearing to.

'She's just a bit too fond of him.'

'I told you. I think you can trust him.'

'Yes but can I trust her? I know she's always been a great one for making up stories, but just lately. . . .'

'Oh she's not herself. It'll pass.'

'No,' said Alice thoughtfully. 'She's not herself at all, is she?'

The *Marie Lamont* was slopping about just off the lighthouse with its sails wrapped around the 'wishbones' at the base of each mast. They had picked up a mooring with Steve showing Tom how to go about it.

'You've never taught me how to do that,' said Liz angrily.

'I can't teach you everything at once Lizzie. Besides this is for your benefit too. It just happens to be a nice calm day today. If you watch you'll learn how it's done.Then you can try next time.'

'Is she OK?' asked Tom anxiously, of the boat.

'I think so.'

'Steve.' Liz tugged at his jersey.

'Wait a minute Lizzie,' he said impatiently. Then to Tom. 'I think that's fine.' He turned back to her. She was behaving like a spoilt child.

'You're not still sick are you?'

'No.' Liz glared at him.

'Right then. What about making us some food?'

'Oh? So I'm not to be a galley slave mm?'

With one part of her mind she despised the way she was behaving but she couldn't stop herself. She would carry on remorselessly and miserably nagging at him until he hated her for it. He was in some measure to blame for he did treat her differently from the way he treated Tom. There was no doubt about it. For some reason Steve was more at ease with Tom. With herself there always seemed to be some physical constraint as though he were half afraid to come close, to touch her. Why? Is it my fault I'm a girl, she thought. But she knew that she was being unreasonable. You think you love him, she told herself. So why shouldn't he feel ill at ease with you? Why can't you just like him and love his boat? Why do all these other feelings come along and complicate matters? Why should a lassie not go to sea?

Liz thought about all this while she made doorstep sandwiches and weak coffee, deliberately contrary. Tom and Steve ate heartily without comment. If they found the meal unappetising they gave no sign. When the sandwiches were finished, Steve took Tom below deck to look at the navigation instruments. Liz had not shown any interest in them. 'Too mathematical,' she had said scowling, with Danny on her mind. She peered through the hatch at the two of them absorbed in technicalities.

'You never showed me the instruments either,' she said accusingly to Steve.

'You always say you aren't interested in maths.' That was Tom.

'I'm not. I hate it.'

'Well Lizzie, this involves a lot of maths,' Steve smiled up at her. Liz grunted.

'So you wouldn't be interested would you?' said Tom with emphasis. They turned their backs on her. 'Pigs,' she thought. 'They're pigs. I hate them, I wish they were dead.'

'You can programme this,' Steve was saying. 'It makes navigation a whole lot simpler. Mind you, when the instruments fail, you have to know what to do, know the calculations to make.'

Liz moved about the deck restless, angry and frustrated. 'I hate you all,' she said, under her breath. She looked up towards the town and the stone. 'I hate you. Why should a lassie not go to sea?'

Her movements had a certain manic air about them. She looked driven, her eyes wild and angry. She opened a locker on deck and took out a bundle of flags. Then she unrolled them and began to run them up the mast.

Ashore two puzzled coastguards were watching the *Marie Lamont* bedecked with flags.

'What the hell is this?' said one. 'Take a look over there.'

'What are they playing at?'

'I'll try to raise them on the radio.' He flicked to Channel Sixteen. '*Marie Lamont. Marie Lamont* this is Clyde Coastguard over.' He repeated the call but there was no reply. Steve and Tom were still engrossed in the instruments below deck, oblivious to Liz's activities above. But the radio was switched off and they could not be contacted.

'That's right,' Steve was saying. 'Now you're getting the hang of it. And if you want to know your projected position in, say, eight hours from now, then. . . .' He pressed several buttons. 'There you are.'

'Great.'

The coastguards gave up trying to contact the yacht. 'Better keep an eye on them though,' said one of the men. 'Just in case.'

Liz looked down into the cabin again. 'Steve,' she said. 'Steve.' But he hardly glanced up. 'Hang on, Liz, I'm busy.'

She clambered on to the foredeck and cast off the mooring. It was not easy but she managed it. The rope cut her fingers. The yacht began to slop about. 'I hate them,' she said aloud. 'Oh how I hate them.' She sat and stared at the shore. A chill little breeze had sprung up from nowhere, blowing from the sea to the land.

Almost imperceptibly at first, the boat began to drift in towards the shore. Soon though, the coastguards spotted the movement.

'He's beginning to drift in.'

'Anyone on deck?'

'Just a wee lassie. Take a look.'

Through the binoculars, they saw Liz standing defiantly on deck now, staring up towards the Granny Kempock Stone.

'Better send a boat out to them. See what's going on.'

Danny was having a drink with some friends in the yacht club, and waiting for Alice to join him. He was still very suspicious of Steve Lamont and wanted to find out more about him. He felt that Alice was weak where Liz was concerned, always giving in to her. He was responsible for the girl as her teacher and now as her potential stepfather too. He felt he must keep an eye on things. But nobody had been able to tell him very much. Henderson, Tom's father, liked the American. 'A good guy,' he said. That at least was something, but nobody seemed to know very much about him: nor where he came from — 'The East Coast' he had said vaguely — nor his ultimate destination. He seemed not to know that himself. Danny, who always knew exactly where he was going felt alarmed by such vagueness. He found it as unnatural as Liz's desire to sail her and lack of interest in boys of her own age. Danny liked everything to be well organised. He liked to know what he was doing this afternoon, tomorrow and preferably this time next year. If he didn't, he felt lost and anxious.

Suddenly everyone seemed to be rushing on to the veranda of the club and looking down towards the bay. He joined them as Alice, late as usual, came rushing in. 'Sorry,' she said. 'Have you been waiting long?'

'Just a few moments. But there's some trouble. A boat in trouble out in the bay.'

'Holiday yachtsmen I expect.'

'No. They believe it's the *Marie Lamont*. Did you let Lizzie go out today?'

'Oh God yes! And with Tom too. What will we do? What will we do?' Danny was intensely irritated. Why did Alice let her daughter do these things and then fly into a panic when something went predictably wrong.

'We'd better wait and see,' he said grimly. 'The inshore lifeboat's just gone out.' I told you so, he thought, his genuine concern for Liz spiced with just a hint of satisfaction at being right. 'I knew that American was bad news,' he thought. 'I knew it.'

Steve was quickly aware of the changed motion of the boat. He rushed up on deck and looked around in astonishment, at the flags. 'What the hell's happening up here?' Then he caught sight of the shoreline, ominously close.'My God we're drifting in. Tom — take the wheel. Take it!' He saw the rocks looming, threatening. There was no time to lose.

'Did it slip?' asked Tom. 'Was it my fault?'

'No it didn't. Liz, what the hell are you playing at?' Steve moved to start the engine pushing Liz roughly aside. She said nothing, her face stony, pale and hard.

Steve was trying desperately to start the engine but with no success. It was quite dead. 'Come on damn you, come on!' he said to it, his customary cool evaporating. He felt the perspiration break out on his brow. 'Come on!' Liz watched him with calm malice. 'It won't start, will it?' she asked and there was a terrible controlled menace in her voice. 'Will it?'

'We're getting really close.' Tom's voice had an edge of panic to it. 'This is all your fault Lizzie!'

'You shouldn't have struck me,' said Liz to Tom.

'What? When did I strike you? What do you mean?'

'I only came to wish you well. What reason was there to strike me?' Ah but you're feart now, aren't you? Feart of a slip of a lassie, aren't you?

'Lizzie!' Steve rapped out the name sharply but she refused to meet his eyes. 'You little bitch,' he said. 'You little bitch!' He caught her by the shoulders and whirled her around to face him so roughly that he almost swept her off her feet. 'Elizabeth Finlay, look at me!' He struck her hard on the face with the flat of his hand. The blow had all the considerable force of his body behind it and the sound of it made Tom wince. Liz reeled under it and would have fallen had he not held her. She cried out, clutching her hand to her cheek. The engine sprang into life. Steve took the wheel from Tom and the boat veered around, away from the rocks, out of danger.

'Jesus' said Steve. 'Oh Jesus Christ!'

'You deserved that,' Tom shouted at Liz. 'You could have killed us all!'

'Tom, come here.' Steve gave him the wheel again then went over to Liz and shook her hard. 'What possessed you to do that? What in God's name possessed you?'

He realised immediately what he had said and stopped short, releasing her. He saw the print of his palm, fiery on her face and the shock in her eyes. She looked at him helplessly, stricken, the blow still ringing in her head. His face loomed over her, dark and threatening, a halo of little pin points of light dancing around it. She flinched away from him. 'It was her,' she whispered. 'Her. Not me. Oh don't hit me again.' Steve stared at her in silence for a moment. She dissolved into tears. 'I'm sorry. Oh Steve I'm sorry. So sorry.'

He pulled her close against him and put his hand gently against her burning cheek, contrite, trying to take away the pain. 'Oh Lizzie, Lizzie, sweet Lizzie, I didn't mean to hurt you. I

113

wouldn't hurt you, you know that. But it was all I could do.'

'I know. I'm sorry.'

Tom, watching, felt uneasily as though the scene he had just witnessed, no matter how shocking, had something passionate and sensual about it. It was indicative of some relationship between them that excluded him totally and angered him, but more than that, he felt a kind of shame for himself and for them.

'Sorry?' he said 'Is that all you can say? Sorry? You could've sunk the boat and us along with it.'

'I know.' Liz's voice was still a whisper. 'But it was her not me. I never meant for it to happen.'

'Who?' asked Tom. 'Are you crazy or what?'

'I think I must be.' She shivered.

'Shut up Tom,' said Steve. His hands were shaking. 'Here.' He took off his jacket, put it around the girl's trembling shoulders and then took the wheel again.

'No harm?' asked Tom indignantly. He had been, however briefly, very frightened and now he was ashamed of himself.

'No,' said Steve. 'No harm done I said.' He gestured to the flags. 'Now hurry up and get these Christmas Tree decorations stowed, all of them.'

Tom, after one look at his skipper's face moved to obey him, but as he passed Liz, he could not resist muttering, 'Why did you do it?'

'Leave her alone,' said Steve, shortly. 'Come on. Jump to it.'

Tom shrugged and began to take down the festooned flags. As the yacht got under way Steve saw the RNLI inflatable approaching them. He groaned. 'More trouble.' He was beginning to appreciate Henderson's warning.

'Ahoy there!' One of the lifeboatmen hailed them, 'What happened?'

'We slipped our mooring,' replied Steve very firmly, and with a warning glance at Tom. He was taking down the last of the flags. Liz stared straight ahead in silence. 'I'm sorry you've had to go to so much trouble.'

'All OK then?'

'Sure. And thanks. I'll buy you a drink, up at the club.'

The man grinned. 'OK. We'll be there.'

As they were securing the *Marie Lamont* at her berth Danny came striding aggressively towards them. Liz saw him as soon as she climbed off the boat.

'What happened?' he demanded.

'Oh it was a false alarm! We slipped a mooring that's all.'
Steve's tone was reassuring. 'And then we couldn't get the engine
started.'

'Sounds pretty dangerous to me,' said Danny.

'No it wasn't. Not really. We got her going just in time.' He
looked at Liz and forced a grin. She gave him a wan little smile in
return. 'You'd better go on home now,' he said to her.

'That's just what she's going to do,' said Danny masterfully.

'Coming Tom?' asked Liz. For once however, Tom was
reluctant to go with her.

'He can stay and have a drink if he likes,' said Steve. 'I mean
you both could. . . .'

'Not Lizzie,' said Danny firmly. He turned to Liz. 'Come on.
Your mum's worried.'

'Well she needn't be. I'm fine. Just fine.'

She walked off keeping one hand over her crimson cheek,
with Danny behind her. Steve watched them go, frowning. He
felt anxious rather than angry and not all his anxiety was for Liz.
'She sure hates him,' he thought. He turned to Tom. 'Come on.
They'll be waiting for us up at the clubhouse.' They tied up the
boat, put springs on her, secured the hatches and hosed her down
all in companionable silence. It was pleasant enough being with
Tom but it certainly lacked some of the spice of Lizzie's company, the sense of never quite knowing what she was going to say
or do next.

In the clubhouse Tom and Steve sat with their two would-be
rescuers. 'Quite a flag day,' said one of the men. 'Cheers.' He
drank Steve's health. 'Mind you, you'll need to have a look at that
engine.'

'I will. I thought I'd got it right.'

'Maybe Liz put the bad eye on it,' ventured Tom.

'Why should you say that?'

'The kids at school call her a witch.' He downed his shandy
with enthusiasm, feeling like a man. 'She plays up to it. She said
she'd ill wished one of the teachers once. I remember his car kept
breaking down. It was weird.'

Why was she such a little misfit thought Steve? Was that the
problem? That she was a square peg in a round hole, so different
from her friends and contemporaries? Or was that detachment
merely a symptom of her condition?

One of the lifeboatmen broke into his thoughts. 'I hear that

115

you're looking for an old schooner?'

'Yes. The *Granny Kempock.*'

'Well,' he said, 'that's her bell up there.' He was pointing to an old brass bell hanging up behind the bar.

'You're kidding!' Steve went closer to look and there, sure enough, was the name *Granny Kempock* engraved on it.

'Well I'll be damned. How did it get here?'

'It used to belong to my father. He gave it to the club.'

'Do you know anything else about her? Like where she went?'

'After she left here? Italy I think.'

'Yes. I heard that she was there.'

'My father worked on her before she went. That's how he had the bell. Present from the German that bought her. He changed the name you see. He had a place somewhere near Ancona. Yes — that was it. Ancona.'

'What did he change her name to?'

'I can't remember. Sorry. And I couldn't say if she's still in Italy either.'

'Never mind. It's something to be going on with anyway. Have another pint.'

Bill Henderson was standing at the bar.

'You're looking pleased with yourself,' he said.

'Yeah, well I found out a little more about my schooner. Where she went when she left Scotland. Italy. Not that she'll still be there, but it's something.'

'Ah,' Henderson nodded. 'So you'll be leaving us.'

'Yes. Yes — I think I'll probably be leaving.'

'I know someone who won't be too pleased about that,' said Henderson with satisfaction.

Steve pretended not to understand. 'Who?'

'Lizzie Finlay. She'll not find anyone daft enough to take her out sailing round here.'

'Why not? She's a good little sailor. She's got enthusiasm — she's bright — she catches on fast.'

'You think?'

'I know. You could do worse than give her a chance.'

'I'll think about it.' Henderson was not convinced but at least, Steve thought, he had sowed a few seeds in his mind. They might eventually bear fruit.

Danny and Liz drove home in silence for most of the journey. Liz, angry and tearful was curled up on the seat beside him, determinedly not looking at him.

'Your mum is worried about you, you know,' said Danny eventually. Anything to force her to speak to him. Her silence unnerved him.

'Oh don't use her as an excuse. You just wanted to spoil everything as usual, didn't you?'

There was a pause while Danny carefully negotiated a roundabout. Then 'Liz,' he said.'Whether you like it or not I'm going to marry your mother.'

Liz didn't reply. Looking sideways at her he saw her scowl. 'I could be fond of you too if you'd let me,' he told her.'Once we got on so well. Why not now?'

'I don't have to like you just because my mother does,' she said. 'I hate you. I wish you were dead.'

'Feel better now you've got that off your chest?'

'No.' It was true. She didn't. Hating him was exhausting. She had to remember to keep it up all the time. To keep on hating him. Sometimes he made her laugh. Sometimes she almost liked him again. Then she had to remind herself that it wasn't allowed. She must just hate him. It tired her out.

At the flat she scrambled out quickly. 'Anyway,' she said, 'I'll not be going back on that boat in a hurry.'

'That's maybe just as well then,' said Danny following her.

'Why?' she stopped.

'Because I — well — your mother and I think that you shouldn't see any more of that man. He's much too old for you.'

'But he's only teaching me to sail.' She was frantic, on the verge of tears again. Danny felt like a monster. But it didn't deter him. He was used to it, used to quelling his own stray dissenting emotions in favour of what he knew to be right. He was very sure of himself. It was his job to enforce rules and regulations.

'Well,' he said sternly, 'that's what we've decided.' He spoke with a deliberate air of finality. 'And you'll just have to accept it. It's for your own good Lizzie.'

'I won't accept anything you say. I'm not a child. And I won't, I won't do as you say.' She rushed on ahead of him into the flat.

Alice hugged her. 'Thank — God you're safe.' Liz submitted woodenly to the embrace.

'What happened?' Alice asked. She held Liz at arm's length.

'Nothing,' Liz was truculent.

'And what happened to your face for goodness sake?' Danny had not noticed but Alice saw the bruise immediately.

117

'Nothing,' Liz repeated. 'I hit it on a hatch cover. Well I mean one fell on me. It's OK. Nothing happened.'

'Oh no. Nothing at all. They were nearly on the rocks. That's all.' Danny followed her in.

'Liz!'

'He says I can't go sailing with Mr Lamont any more. With Steve. Tell him I can mum. Tell him I can.'

Alice twisted her hands nervously together. 'But I think he may be right Liz.'

She whirled around to her grandmother.

'Gran?'

'It's no good asking me now,' said Rose.

'Why not?' asked Liz furiously. 'You've always looked after me. You've always been the one to decide what I can and can't do. Why should it suddenly be him? He has no right!'

Alice was stung by the taunt. 'He has every right.'

'Anyway, Rose won't always be here,' said Danny. Better to have it out in the open now. Rose groaned inwardly.

'What do you mean? What's wrong?'

'Why now Danny?' thought Rose. 'In God's name why now?'

'Nothing's wrong Lizzie. It's just that I'm thinking of getting my own flat. That's all.'

'And I'll be here instead,' put in Danny. 'Oh you'll soon get used to it.'

Much as he liked her he had been relieved to learn of Rose's planned move. It was going to be difficult enough for him, having to cope with Lizzie after the wedding without having his mother-in-law breathing down his neck as well. That was how he put it to himself.

'I won't be far away,' said Rose soothingly. 'It won't make all that much difference you know.'

'Oh won't it!' Liz turned on Danny. 'Listen you. You can't tell me what to do any more. I'm sixteen. I won't go back to school to be taught by you and I won't stop sailing for you. You can't rule my life any more, any of you.'

She was already at the door.

'Liz,' said Danny 'You come back here this minute!'

'No,' said Liz. 'I won't. You can go to hell. All of you.' They heard the outside door slam behind her.

'Now that was really tactful,' said Rose but Danny had had enough. He had deliberately tried to hurt Liz. Why should she have it all her own way?

118

'I'm sick of all this,' he said. 'It's always Liz and her feelings in this house. Well I've got feelings too. Do you think it doesn't hurt when she tells me she hates me? How do you think that makes me feel? Mm? Do you think I'm made of stone or something?'

Liz was beside Granny Kempock, sobbing and gasping for breath. 'They won't stop me,' she cried. 'Not this time. I'll see them in hell first. They'll have to burn me to stop me now!'

MARIE: 1662

Soon after I was well again my Thomas was married in the kirk to Janet McKenzie and when I went to offer him my hand and wish him luck of the match, long life and happiness, he struck me hard on the face so that blood poured from my mouth.

Then I hated him and I went up to Kempock with Kettie Scott, Janet Holm and some others where we intended to cast the lang-stane into the sea, whereby to destroy a wheen boats and ships and hinder men frae killing the fish. We danced and the devil kissed us but we could not shift the stane.

Still, the next day a great storm blew up which I do believe we were the cause of and my Thomas was drowned. I call him my Thomas though truly he was Janet McKenzie's Thomas and I am sorry for her. It was me that found him, lying drowned on the seashore his poor body all tangled with sea wrack, like rags and his oilskins in shreds from the pounding of the great rocks. And when I saw his poor body I repented of all my ill doing. Folk were whispering that I was a witch and that Kettie was the chief and ringleader who had led me into sin and I knew they spoke the truth.

Kettie had been as a mother to me and I loved her dearly but when I told her of Thomas and his body there on the shore she only laughed at me and said I was a fond foolish lassie. And did I not have a better lover now than a silly fisher lad and why was I not content?

And then God moved my heart to confess because I have been long in the devil's service. And so I tell't them. I tell't them every-thing. They took me to Glasgow to stand trial with Kettie and Janet Holm and the others.

I half thought my maister might come to me in the prison where they held me but he did not. What else could I expect since I have so rejected him?

I hear the curses of the other women ringing in my ears still. They do not call me a fond foolish lassie now. I think that there is nobody in the whole wide world who loves me. I find hatred on all sides. And then I repent me of my treachery to my friends. But what else can I do? If I am to save my immortal soul, what else can I do?

7

Liz awoke on Friday morning with anger still heavy in her heart.
Her head ached dully and when she looked at herself in the mirror it seemed as if the skin of her face was stretched thin and frail
across her high wide cheekbones while a pair of dark haunted
eyes stared back at her.

She blamed them all: Danny for being so stern and unbending;
Alice for being weak and submitting to him; Rose for not taking
her part when she knew how much sailing meant to her. Even
Steve, for his apparent indifference. All of them were to blame
and somebody would have to pay. She sat in the room and stared
at the lizard and thought black thoughts until presently her mind
became empty and then she thought of nothing at all. Her eyes
were blank. She might have been totally absent though a watcher
would have become uneasily aware of another and more sporadic presence: someone who also peered out at the world with
fear and hatred, with a frustrated longing that had survived the
centuries, with an ambition that flickered occasionally into life
as a fire may flare up when it is thought to be long extinguished. A
watcher may have seen all this but there was no watcher and only
the lizard saw.

Rose and Alice sat at the kitchen table and drank tea. Danny
had gone back to his own small flat. He was planning to sell it in
time for the wedding and move into Alice's home.

'Do you think we should call a doctor?' said Alice. Danny had
bought her a ring, a large sapphire. She had twisted it round and
round her finger in her anxiety until the skin had become red and
inflamed underneath it. She ought to be so happy but Liz was
spoiling everything, deliberately it seemed.

'No, I don't think that's necessary. She needs someone to treat
her like an adult for a change,' said Rose patiently. Somehow
something had to be salvaged from this mess. For a long time, she
had a conviction that everything would come right in the end, a
conviction that was somehow connected with Steve Lamont, the
American. Why, she wondered? A breath of New World air, perhaps? Still she had lately begun to doubt that intuition, so
strange had Liz's behaviour become.

'We do treat her like an adult, don't we?' Alice voice trailed off querulously.

'Well, no. Danny doesn't. Oh I know she doesn't always behave like an adult either and I know Danny has the best of intentions, but, well, he's so heavy handed. So much the teacher. I don't suppose he can help it.'

'Then what do you suggest?'

'Well — she's obsessed by the sea. She needs to sail like nothing else. Why don't you take that seriously for a start?'

'But we can't afford it.'

'Oh nonsense. You've got it into your head that sailing's expensive. It needn't be. There are all sorts of possibilities.'

'Such as?'

'Well she could join a club, have dinghy sailing lessons, go on a sailing holiday. You could afford that. I could help out. You'll have Danny's money coming in too.'

'I never thought about it,' said Alice.

'Well you should have. I didn't really give it much thought till now either. But that's what she needs. Give her that and this American and his yacht won't seem half so important, believe me.'

The telephone in the hall rang, startling them and Alice went to answer it. In her bedroom Liz heard the strident bell but ignored it. She had taken the lizard out of his cage and was holding it, talking to it.

'It's all going wrong again,' she said. 'How can I stop it?' She took the little creature over to the window and looked down towards the sea. But do I want to stop it, she thought. Do I really want to?

In the hallway Alice was talking over the phone to Tom. 'I'll try and persuade her,' she told him. 'But you know what she's like.' Tom evidently did know all too well. 'Wait a minute,' she said. She put down the receiver and knocked on Liz's bedroom door. 'Phone,' she said.

'Tell them I'm not here.'

Alice went back. 'I'll ask her,' she said. 'I'll try.' She hung up and came into Liz's room.

'That was Tom. He wanted to speak to you.'

'Well I don't want to speak to him. I hate him.'

'You mustn't say that Liz.'

'Why not?'

'Well — it hurts people.'

'They hurt me, don't they?'

122

Alice decided to try another tack. 'There's a party on this evening. He wants you to go.'

'No. I don't want to.'

'I said you might. Oh Lizzie, do go. You'll probably enjoy it.'

'Do you mean I'm actually allowed to go out all on my own. Gosh, what does Danny say to that?'

'Oh don't be silly.'

'But you don't trust me.'

'Yes we do.'

'Anyway,' said Liz with a faint spark of interest.'Who's going? Did he say?'

'Some of your friends from school. People from the sailing club.'

So Steve might just possibly be there. Not much hope, but still a glimmer. 'I don't care if I never see him again,' she had raged, but she did, she did.

'It's a barbecue down at the shore,' said Alice hopefully.

'Well I might go.' She looked at her mother's anxious face and felt tears gathering in her eyes. I'm behaving so badly. I make myself and everyone so miserable. Why? Because I can't help it. Because I'm not myself. But then who am I? She had a glimpse of the precipice in her head, the gaping chasm into which she might tumble, never to crawl out again. She was so frightened. Only Steve seemed to realise just how frightened she was, seemed able to dispel that fear, and now he had chosen to abandon her, discouraged by Danny. Why did everyone bow to Danny's wishes?

'I might go,' she said, squeezing her mother's hand.

At the marina Steve was passing Henderson's boatyard on his way back to the *Marie Lamont*. He was wheeling one of the marina trolleys, piled high with provisions, which he had just unloaded from a hire car. There were tins of meat and vegetables, packets of dried goods, loaves of bread, cartons of long life milk.

'I see you're on your way again,' said Bill Henderson.

'Yes that's right. I thought I might stay longer but — well — I've got itchy feet, you know? I'll be off as soon as I get the engine checked over.'

'Think you'll find your *Granny Kempock* this time?'

'I hope so. I've got to try. I've come this far. It'll be worth it if I find her.'

Henderson gestured at his old fishing boat. 'You might like to buy this one when she's ready. For your museum. At a price.'

'I just might,' said Steve, laughing. 'At a price. How about a drink later?'

'In the club?' asked Henderson. 'OK?'

Steve trundled his barrow contentedly off down the pontoon. He loved all the preparations for a voyage.

He felt the familiar excitement gripping him. Time to move on. He had been here long enough and as usual he was going to leave it all behind him.

Sometimes when he thought about this in himself he saw it as a kind of moral cowardice but he never felt sufficiently strongly about it to try to change himself. He was a natural drifter, and if, as a rolling stone he gathered no moss, who needs moss?'

He had tried the rat race, the conventional nine to five mode of existence once or twice, but he couldn't even bear the sailing school for longer than six months at a time. As far as he was concerned he might as well be dead as settled down and so, when he thought about his journey he felt the joy rise in him once more.

In the early evening Liz put on her red dress, the same dress that she had worn on her visit to Glasgow with Steve. She always felt good in it. It looked right with her pale skin and black hair. Then she made up her face very carefully. In his cage, the lizard watched her as she deftly applied eyeshadow and blusher. It was not often that she could be bothered with such trappings. Normally she professed to despise them, but, like most girls, she had experimented in the privacy of her room and Danny would have been amazed by her expertise.

The sun was descending over the far hills, through a bank of cloud, sky and sea below it taking on a lurid red hue. Shepherd's delight, she thought. The red was the colour of her dress. The whole room was burning and only her face in the mirror looked palely back at her. Her hand holding the mascara brush slipped, streaking black down her cheek like a sooty tear. 'Damn,' she said and wiped it off. Steadying herself she continued to paint her face until she was satisfied. The girl that looked back at her could have been any age between fifteen and twenty five. She had masked herself with an oddly theatrical beauty. The skin was smooth alabaster, the lips just tinged with crimson, the eyes large and emphatic.

An engineer was making minor adjustments, aboard the *Marie Lamont*. Steve was planning to leave early the next day. Very early. He would just slip away with no fuss. When Liz came down to the marina the boat would be gone. She would be angry and disappointed but perhaps that was all to the good. She would think the less of him for it. He regretted not being able to say goodbye to her more than he cared to admit even to himself. His feeling for her was more than just an attraction towards a young, pretty girl. They had recognised some fundamental similarity, some compatibility in each other. They were kindred spirits. But though he was free, she was young with all the ties of home and family still restraining her. He could do nothing about it and it would be better by far for her to forget him. He would send her a nice postcard from wherever he made his next landfall; perhaps keep in touch from a safe distance until out of sight finally became out of mind.

'What was wrong then?' he asked the engineer.

'Well if I'm being honest with you I couldn't find anything at all to account for her not starting like that. But then you never know, do you? Could be sand in the fuel. Anyway, she's in fine shape now. No problem.'

'Another mystery eh?'

'Just like a woman. That's what I alway say.'

The young people of the town youth club had built a huge bonfire on the upper part of a fine stretch of beach, just beyond the marina, where little dry grasses poked through and rustled in the evening wind. They had brought a portable cassette player and somebody had lent a big barbecue. There were sausages and hamburgers, a big pan of fried onions and a tray of split rolls. There were jars of tomato sauce and mustard and potatoes ready wrapped in tinfoil, to go in the embers of the fire.

A motley collection of the teenagers of the town were gathered around the fire: some dancing, some standing in groups, and some sitting comfortably on the short turf.

Liz wandered rather hesitantly up to the party. She had lived in the town all her life and knew the vast majority of the people here, at least by sight. Most of them were friends. So why did she feel so odd and alienated? It was as if a glass partition had snapped down separating her from them, or one of those invisible force fields common to science fiction and fairy stories. She was enchanted and could not join them. Some of the younger members of the Cruising Club were gathered in a group drinking wine and beer. They were the young men that Tom scathingly called the 'boy racers' and their girlfriends were smart and self

125

confident in white oilskin jackets and designer jeans, their voices ringing with assurance.

Nowhere could she see Steve although she scanned the faces anxiously for a glimpse of him. Instead she saw Tom, elbowing his way through the crowd towards her, with a big bottle of cider. 'Hi,' he said. 'I'm glad you came, Lizzie.'

'I nearly didn't.'

'Trouble at home?' he asked sympathetically.

'A bit.'

'Have some cider. Make you feel better.'

He filled a paper cup for her and was alarmed by the speed with which she gulped it down. 'Here,' he cautioned her. 'Slow down can't you?'

'More,' she said, holding out her cup.

'Are you sure?' Tom was doubtful. He knew that Liz drank the occasional glass of wine at home, but this was different.

'Hurry up then!' She jiggled his elbow. 'You don't have to be responsible for me you know. I'll be responsible for myself thank you. Now — give me some more.'

Cowed, he poured her another cup. A faint cheer went up, the crowds swirled around them and parted to reveal a thin plume of smoke curling up from the bonfire. 'So they've built a fire,' she said.

'I like your dress.' Tom edged closer. 'The colour really suits you, Lizzie.' He seldom noticed her clothes but he was making a determined effort to be nice to her.

She turned back to him. 'A bonny red gown,' she said. Her heart had begun to pound so that she was sure he must hear the wild thudding. There was to be no escape then. They were lighting a fire for her. Tom began to move closer to it, pulling her with him. What was he trying to do? He stopped as he encountered her resistance. 'I didn't know,' she said. 'I didn't know about the bonfire.' Her head swivelled around, scanning the crowds.

'Are you looking for someone?' asked Tom suspiciously.

'Steve. Mr Lamont. I thought he might be here.'

'No. He won't be here. He's got other things to do tonight.'

'What things? Have you seen him?'

'Well my dad has. Not me. But would it matter if I had seen him? It's a free country Lizzie. He isn't your property. I can talk to the man if I want to.'

So Steve, her one port in the storm that threatened to overwhelm her, had abandoned her. Kate came up and took Tom's arm. 'Hi Lizzie,' she said. 'Come closer to the fire. Come on.' Why was Tom pulling at her, Liz wondered hazily? Did he hate her so much? Why did he want to pull her into the flames? And then the thought struck her: but he's dead, isn't he? He's drowned. I saw him on the beach. She recoiled in horror from his touch, staring at him.

'Lizzie?' he said, puzzled. 'Come on Lizzie.' 'No,' she thought with relief. 'That was another Tom. Another time.'

Kate dropped his arm impatiently. 'You're a dead loss,' she told him, and joined a group of her friends. Liz moved to stand with her back to the fire. She felt better when she couldn't see it though she could hear the crackle and roar of the flames as they soared up behind her. The cider too was singing in her head.

'Gosh,' said Tom. 'You can feel the heat from here.'

'I can't breathe.' The smoke was in her mouth and in her nostrils, but she couldn't move.

'Are you all right?'

'It's the fire. I don't like the flames. I hate the flames.'

'But you used to love bonfires, when we were kids. Don't you remember Lizzie? It was always me who was afraid of fireworks, not you. You used to love the bonfire on Guy Fawkes night, and the rockets and everything. Don't you remember?'

'They burnt people on fires you know,' said Liz. 'Here on this shore.'

'Burnt people?'

'Witches.'

She smoothed her dress down. 'A bonny red gown. A sheet of flame like a bonny red gown.'

Another of Liz's schoolfriends, Jen, came up to them. 'I haven't seen you for ages Liz,' she said. 'Where have you been hanging out then?'

'She's been sailing,' said Tom. He couldn't keep the note of scorn out of his voice.

'Not any more though,' said Liz, and her eyes had gone blank again. 'They won't let me now, will they? I hate them. You don't know how much I hate them all.'

The girl did not know what to make of this, nor of the face that Tom pulled behind Liz's back, so she ignored it completely.

'It's a great fire, isn't it?' she said. 'We're going to bake potatoes.' She wandered off. 'Coming?' she said over her shoulder as she went.

'Soon,' said Tom. 'In a minute.'

'A great fire,' said Liz. 'A great fire.' She turned again to look at the bonfire. She saw a crowd of people laughing and jeering, shaking their fists and spitting at her. She could hear oaths and catcalls. The flames roared higher, yellow, blue and crimson. And was that a figure in the midst of them?

'She was taken and burnt in a great fire on the seashore near her home,' whispered Liz. She covered her face with her hands. The flames crept closer, the terrible stench of burning flesh filling her nostrils. How they hated her. And how she hated them. Maybe she had confessed of her own free will, but now she hated them. She would die, hating them. The flames were like her hatred, consuming her. Soon there would be nothing left of her at all.

She crouched there on the seashore, huddled into herself, hands over her face. She was rocking backwards and forwards, in agony, moaning gently to herself. Tom was trying desperately to pull her to her feet. She was embarrassing him. He would have walked away from her, if he dared, but he couldn't quite bring himself to desert her.

'What on earth's wrong with her?' asked Jen. 'Is she all right?'

Kate was callous. 'She's been weird for days.' Jen's boyfriend turned away impatiently. He didn't know Liz and he didn't care about her very much. 'Looks as if she ought to be on the funny farm to me,' he said. 'Come on. Let's put some more spuds on.'

Jen was still concerned but reluctant to get involved. She had never been over fond of Liz anyway. 'OK,' she said. 'I just wondered, that's all.'

'He drowned you see,' said Liz, half to herself.

'Who?' Tom was still hot with embarrassment. 'People are looking at us Lizzie,' he said. 'Oh get up Lizzie please!' He was very much afraid. He wished that Steve were here. Steve would know what to do.

'He drowned,' said Liz in great distress. 'She pushed the stone and she cursed him anyway and because the stone was old and powerful and because her heart was full of hatred, he died. But she didn't mean for him to drown. They said I did. But I never meant for him to drown. They said I put an ill cast on him. Listen to how they hate me. They're screaming at me. God forgive me, I gave myself to the devil. I did too.' Her vision suddenly wavered. The bonfire shimmered in the haze from its own heat. 'Oh but I never meant for Tom to drown.'

She was walking along the seashore. The sand glittered with

128

an unnatural light, dazzling her. Ahead of her was a body lying face down, seaweed twined around it. She reached out and grasped it. It was soft and spongy and a terrible smell arose from it. With a great effort she managed to turn it over. The body was sodden and heavy with water like a great rag doll. Flies rose in a little cloud. She looked at the face. It was Tom's face, almost unrecognisable, bloated, drowned and dead. She had known it all along. She began to wipe her hand convulsively up and down her skirt, up and down, up and down, trying to wipe away the nauseous feel of drowned flesh.

'I never meant for Tom to drown,' she said.

'Tom?' he asked bewildered. 'Me? What do you mean?'

'Tom?' she repeated. 'Oh no. Not you. Oh Tom!'

Thinking she was calling to him and aware only of her distress he put his arms around her to comfort her. He kissed her gently, shocked for a moment out of his customary clumsiness.

'Not you!' she said, clinging close to him. She snuggled into him and was comforted for a moment but then over his shoulder she saw the fire blazing brightly. She could hear the cries of the crowd. They were dancing around it and singing. She wrenched herself away from him.

'No,' she said. 'Don't touch me. It's no good. Nothing changes. Look at the fire. Look at the flames.'

This was too much for Tom. He had drunk the best part of a bottle of cider. He lost his temper. 'I don't know where I am with you,' he said. 'One minute you're all over me and the next you're saying you hate me. Just who do you think you are?'

'I don't know,' said Liz, but he ignored her, too intent on his own misery.

'Just because you can get some daft American to take you out on his boat . . . sailor? You're no sailor. You'll never be a sailor. You're just a stupid girl and you'll never be any good at it.'

The tirade brought Liz back to herself.

'Well what about you?' she spat at him. 'You say you want to be fisherman? You know nothing about the sea. I'm a hundred times better than you are. You're hopeless at everything. Everything!'

'I'm not hopeless Lizzie. I'm not!'

Liz laughed at him coarsely. It scarcely sounded like Lizzie at all. 'You'll be sorry for this,' she said. 'You'll be sorry for striking me.'

'But I didn't hit you. It was Steve. Not me. Don't you

129

remember.'

'Look!' She brought her hand away and he saw, incredulously, that there was blood on it and on her mouth.

'I come to wish you luck and this is what you do to me,' she said. 'Well you'll be sorry.'

'To wish me luck? Are you mad or what? Listen Liz Finlay, I can handle a boat better than a lassie any day of the week. And I'll prove it to you. I'll prove it to you now.'

He turned and ran off in the direction of the harbour. Liz watched him go. 'What have I done?' she thought.

Kate came up behind her.

'What's got into him?' she asked curiously. 'Where's he going?'

'I didn't mean it.'

'But what did you say to him? Where's he off to?'

Liz was wholly herself again. 'No,' she said. 'Oh my God no. He mustn't go. He'll drown. I know he will. He'll drown!'

She set off at a run, towards the marina and the yacht club. The flames flared behind her and there was a whoop of devilment as somebody lifted a potato on a stick, high out of the fire. Liz heard the cry, and ran on through the twilight.

Tom had already reached the marina, his head full of cider, rejection and anger. Up on the hard-standing he found a new Laser dinghy. With a great deal of difficulty he managed to launch it. His rage seemed to lend him strength. He was determined to prove himself. 'I'll show her,' he kept thinking. 'I'll just show her, so I will,' and then, childishly 'But she'll be sorry. Oh she'll be sorry.'

In the yacht club bar Steve was having a last drink with Tom's father.

'All set?' Bill Henderson asked.

'Just about. I'll be back to buy that bell one of these days. And maybe your boat too Bill.'

'You'll make us both offers we can't refuse, eh?' said the barman. He was washing and drying glasses when the phone rang. The bar was quiet except for Steve, Bill Henderson and three yachtsmen drinking beer, at a corner table. Just as the barman picked up the phone, Liz came running in. Her heart sank when she saw Henderson talking to Steve. 'Excuse me,' she said.

'You're not supposed to be in here at all,' said Henderson severely.

'Out!' said the barman, covering the mouthpiece with his

hand. 'You're under age.'

'I need your help,' she said urgently to Steve, willing him to understand.

'Is this another of your stories?' he asked, but his heart had risen at the sight of her.

The barman put the phone down and called across to one of the yachtsmen at the corner table. 'Jeff Sutherland,' he said, 'someone's been seen taking your dinghy out. A young lad. Do you know about it?'

'No. I bloody well do not!' Sutherland leapt to his feet and rushed out of the bar. 'Kids!' he said as he went. 'I'll murder them.'

'Where was it?' Steve asked the barman.

'Just drawn up on the hard between the harbour and the marina I think. That's where he usually keeps his boat. New this season. It'll be some young tearaway.'

'Come outside please.' Liz tugged at his jacket. 'Come outside and I'll tell you.'

Steve got up. 'Come on then,' he said to Liz and strode out.

'That girl's a menace. Somebody should do something about her.' Henderson shook his head, downed his pint and ordered another.

Out on the water a little evening wind had whipped up small waves and Tom was finding it increasingly difficult to control the dinghy. It was a bigger and more sophisticated craft than his little Mirror, far more headstrong and unstable. He was not a strong swimmer and he was not wearing a lifejacket either, but the look of grim determination had not left his face. With every move he made the boat rocked more dangerously. It was growing dark and the water around the boat looked soupy and menacing.

Liz had told Steve the full story, clearly and succinctly. No time for histrionics, he thought, approvingly, though she seemed almost demented with fear and guilt. 'I didn't mean for him to do it,' she kept saying. 'I never meant for him to do it. You know that don't you?'

Steve cut into her recriminations. 'Have you got any idea where he'd be going?'

'Oh I don't know. Yes I do.' She froze. 'To Dunoon. Sometimes the lads try to swim there. Sometimes they drown.'

Steve saw the strange preoccupied look threatening to engulf her again. 'Liz,' he said. 'You've got to stop this nonsense. Pull yourself together.' He shook her, roughly. 'Do you hear me?'

'Yes,' she said. 'Yes, I hear you.'

'Right.' He was at the wheel of the *Marie Lamont*. They had cast off and were soon motoring out into the channel. 'Inflate the dinghy,' he told her. 'Quickly.'

'What for?'

'No questions. Do it.' He glanced at her. '*Can* you do it?'

She rose to the doubt in his voice. 'Of course I can.'

She took the footpump and began to inflate the rubber tender.

Out in the main channel Tom, in a sudden and miscalculated attempt to change direction while trying to avoid a piece of floating debris, capsized the Laser.

The boom struck him awkwardly on the arm as it swung round and down. There was a sickening crack as metal made contact with bone. He went under, gasping with pain and almost losing consciousness but the cold water shocked him awake. He bobbed to the surface, shook the water from his eyes and managed to cling to the upturned boat.

Liz, on Steve's instructions, was scanning the sea and the darkening horizon. 'Can you see him?' he asked. They were towing the tender behind them. It bounced up and down as they motored along.

'I thought I could just now, but I've lost him again.'

'Keep your eyes on the sea,' said Steve sharply. 'The place where you last saw him. Do you have it?'

'Yes. I think so. Yes.'

'Well point.'

'Point?'

'Yes. Point at it, for God's sake. It's the best indication we have. Point and keep on pointing. Right?'

'Like this?'

'Right. Keep on like that. I don't give a damn if your arm aches. Just keep on pointing.'

At the party, word had got around that Tom was out on the water. No-one was quite sure in what: some said a rowing boat, some a dinghy, some that he was trying to swim. The party had lost its spirit. The group from the yacht club had gone on to better things. The fire was dying down and people stood about in small groups looking out to sea. A few were busying themselves with gathering up litter into big plastic bin bags: paper cups, the remains of hamburgers, Coke tins and cigarette packets.

Kate and Jim stood apart from all the rest, staring apprehensively out across the water.

'It's her fault,' said Kate. 'Liz drove Tom to do that. If he drowns, it'll be all her fault.'

Liz was still pointing at the place where she had last seen Tom and the floating dinghy. Distant waves masqueraded briefly as human heads, only to dissolve into empty sea and she was beginning to despair until she realised that one had resolved itself quite definitely into a boat with a figure clinging to it.

'Over there!' she cried.

'Where?'

'There. Look. He's in the water. The boat's capsized.'

'You're right. Good girl.'

As they motored closer, she called out to Tom and he managed to wave to them feebly, almost losing his grip on the dinghy as he did so.

'He's conscious,' said Steve. 'That's good. Never mind waving!' he shouted. 'We see you. Just hang on.'

Steve cut the engine, got into the rubber dinghy and, taking a line with him, motored over to Tom, leaving Liz in charge of the *Marie Lamont*. It helped that the boy was still conscious. It would have been the devil of a job if he had passed out.

'I think my arm's broken,' said Tom.

'Looks that way to me. Hold on. Now hang on to my arm with your good arm,' said Steve. 'That's it. I've got you. Now listen to me and listen good.' He spoke urgently and emphatically. 'You're going to feel me pushing you down. OK?' Tom nodded. 'I'm not trying to drown you so for God's sake don't panic and struggle or you'll have us both in the water. But it's the only way to get you into the boat. You're too heavy otherwise. I'll push you under. You'll shoot up like a porpoise and I can haul you in. OK? Do you understand Tom?'

Again Tom nodded.

'Take a deep breath now. . .'

'Oh God,' said Tom. The pain in his arm was agonising. Holding his breath, he felt a pair of strong arms thrusting him down hard, by the shoulders, felt a sudden knife of pain, under the pressure and then the great power of the water was pushing him up, up and out and he was in the dinghy, landed like a great fish, sprawling, panting for breath with Steve leaning over him.

'Thank God for that,' he heard the American say, close to his

133

ear. Steve motored back to the *Marie Lamont*, shortening the tow rope as he went. From the rubber dinghy, he shouted up to Liz. 'Looks like his arm's broken. I won't try to tow the Laser as well. Someone else can rescue that. We'd best get him ashore as soon as we can.' He looked up speculatively, at Liz. 'Listen, I can't get him aboard without doing him more damage. Do you think you can take her in? Tow us behind?'

Liz didn't answer at once. 'Throw me that blanket,' said Steve. He wrapped the shivering Tom up in it. 'Well?' he asked again. 'I'll shout instructions to you. You can do it.'

'Do you think so?'

'Yes I do.'

'All right,' she said quietly. 'I'll do it.'

'I'm sorry Liz. Lizzie,' muttered Tom as he finally slipped into unconsciousness but only Steve heard him.

'Right,' said Steve briskly. 'Steer for the lighthouse, OK?'

'Yes. I'll be fine. Just fine.' She turned around and slipped the engine in gear her fingers trembling. Then she took the wheel and guided the boat surely and safely into the marina.

Many people saw Liz bringing in the *Marie Lamont* that night, with a great deal of amazement. They included the coast-guards,the ambulancemen waiting on the quayside and Bill Henderson who didn't know whether to be angry or grateful. The Mackenzies who had just arrived for the weekend, watched her with pride. 'That's our Lizzie,' said Mr Mackenzie, to anyone who would listen. 'She's a great friend of ours. She's often on our boat.'

Liz, standing proudly up at the helm looked as if she had been reborn. At the marina she even managed to berth the *Marie Lamont* single handed. Willing hands caught the warps and one of the marina officials leapt aboard to help her tie up.'That was well done,' he said warmly and patted her on the back. 'I wouldn't have believed you had it in you, lass. But I'm glad. Well done.'

Steve had cast off the tender and ferried Tom directly to the steps by the shore. His father was waiting there with the ambulance crew. Tom came round in the ambulance to see Bill Henderson sitting watching him, his brow furrowed with worry. He looked old and grey.

'I thought you were a gonner there son.'

'Not me.' Tom closed his eyes for a moment or two, then

opened them and looked directly at his father.

'Dad?'

'What?'

'I'm going to the fishing. Just as soon as I can get a place on a boat. I'll start as cook if anyone'll have me.'

'We'll talk about it later.'

'No. There's nothing to talk about. I've made up my mind. I'm going to the fishing. I've only got one life and that's what I want to do with it. If I don't try it I'll always regret it. So I'm going to the fishing.'

The Mackenzies had come down to the pontoon and hugged Liz as she clambered off the boat. She walked round to the steps with them and then stood with Steve to watch Tom being driven away in the ambulance. A police car followed.

'He'll be OK now,' said Steve.

'But will he get into trouble?' Liz was worried. 'I mean about the boat. He nicked it. I feel responsible.'

'Well — probably — but they'll find it and bring it in. Someone's out now, looking for it. No great harm done. I had a word with Bill Henderson. The owner's a friend of his it seems. I don't think anything too serious will come of it all.'

'It was my fault.'

'Stop blaming yourself. Tom pinched the boat not you. His dad'll put things straight. And anyway, you did a great job. I didn't know you had it in you Lizzie.'

'Well I have,' she said happily. 'I have.'

Automatically they had started to walk back to the boat together but then Steve recollected himself and stopped on the pontoon. He caught her hand and turned her to face him. What would he say? She held her breath. 'Liz,' he said. 'I've had definite news about my *Granny Kempock*. My schooner. So I'm going to Italy to look for her.'

Come with me, he was going to ask her. Sail with me. She willed him to say it but he didn't.'I've got to go and look for her,' he told her.

'I see. When?'

'Tomorrow.'

'Tomorrow?'

She had thought he was going to say next week, next month perhaps. He saw the colour leave her face but there was no help for it. No help for her. 'I wish I could go with you,' she said.

135

He laughed. She hated him for laughing. 'No more daydreams now,' he said. Even after all she had done he still thought of her as a child.

'I'm not dreaming. I could crew for you. I could help you. You just said I did a good job. Nobody wants me here. Oh let me come with you.'

'Lizzie, Lizzie.' He hugged her but it meant nothing. 'This is the Clyde honey. Not the open sea. And anyway, what would Danny say to that eh?'

'Him? What does he matter?'

What could he offer her by way of consolation. 'Look,' he said, 'maybe when you're older. . . . I'll keep in touch. I promise. You might get to the States some day. See our museum.'

She was inconsolable. She had helped him to rescue Tom but what did that matter? She was as far as ever from realising her ambitions.

'Will I see you again before you go?' she asked, clutching at straws. 'I'd like to see you before you leave.'

'Better not I think. I need an early start. I'll be leaving at dawn. You can give me a wave from your bedroom window if you like!' He ruffled her hair affectionately. 'I'll send you some postcards kid, I promise.' He fished inside his jacket pocket and handed her a little printed card. 'That's the sailing school. Write to me, why don't you? Care of that address. Let me know how you get on.'

She took the card, resisting the impulse to toss it in the water. She knew that she would regret the gesture later on. There was a lump in her throat as she turned to leave. 'Goodbye then,' she said and walked away very fast. Steve felt curiously desolate to see her go. It was as though he were leaving unfinished business, and although he was used to sailing away, like the good seaman he was, he disapproved of loose ends, liked to leave things shipshape behind him.

Liz said nothing to Alice and Rose about the rescue. They would hear about it soon enough. Danny would be sure to find out about it and disapprove of all that she had done. She went to bed very early and wet her pillow with weeping. The love inside her wrenched at her like a physical pain but she could not tell whether it was longing for the man or the boat or perhaps for both together.

In his cage the lizard flickered restlessly from stone to stone. Liz slept until the moon rose and shone in at her window. It seemed to rouse her for she sat up suddenly. Then she got out of bed and began to move purposefully about the room.

Very early on Saturday morning Steve was up and about aboard the *Marie Lamont,* preparing to leave. A little tingle of fear spiced his excitement. Single handing was always unpredictable. You never knew what crises you might be called upon to meet. That was half the fun of it as far as he was concerned. He loved to be his own master and if that meant taking risks then so much the better. Sometimes it was necessary to taste danger just to prove to yourself that you were alive. He left the marina with only one backward glance and that was up towards the stone, up towards Liz's house.

Once he was well out into the bay, he went into the small fore-cabin in search of some piece of equipment and noted in passing that he didn't remember having left the hatch as wide open as all that. Under a pile of sails something, somebody lay curled up, sleeping peacefully. It was Elizabeth Finlay.

She had crept aboard in the early hours of the morning and had lain there hardly daring to breathe until the throbbing of the engine and delicate motion had sent her, like a baby, off to sleep.

Steve's immediate reaction was one of intense anger. He shook her awake. 'Liz,' he said. 'Of all the dumb things!' She stared up at him, disorientated for a moment. He turned his back on her and went up on deck, seeking to control his temper. She had not seen him so furious before.

'You crazy kid. Of all the crazy kids I've ever known. . . . God Lizzie, you're asking for it, aren't you? I ought to toss you over the side and let you swim for home!' He frightened her again. Rubbing her eyes like a child she followed him up on deck. He was furling in the sails.

'I'm not a kid,' she said, defiantly. 'I've run away. I'm coming with you. I'm old enough. They can't stop me. There's not a thing they can do.'

'Maybe they can't do anything,' he said. 'But I sure as hell as can.' He had lost patience. Enough was enough. He started the engine.

'Wait,' she cried in anguish. 'Oh please. Don't take me back.'

'I must,' said Steve.

'Well not yet.' She pulled at him in desperation. 'Please not yet. Look, I have to talk to you. Honestly.'

He turned off the engine again.

'OK. So talk.' He looked at his watch. 'I give you five minutes. Then we go back in. Your family's going to lynch me as it is Lizzie. Her face scrubbed clean of yesterday's makeup was pale with fatigue and she looked young and vulnerable. The boat slopped about in the path of the rising sun. The water dappled in little golden ripples about them. Steve waited.

'I'll try to explain,' said Liz. 'Once and for all. Just listen to me and I'll try.'

Alice, going sleepily into Liz's room with a cup of tea found the empty bed and the note. The piece of scrimshaw was gone. Jeans, teeshirts and sweaters were missing from the wardrobe.

'Gran, please look after my lizard, said the note. 'I have to go away. I'm sorry mum. I'll write.'

Alice rushed in to wake Rose. 'She's gone,' she said. 'This time she's gone. She really has. Look. She's left a note.'

'Does she say where?'

'No. Just away.'

'Get dressed,' said Rose. 'I think I might know where she is.'

'Where?'

'I think Steve Lamont's got a stowaway. I wonder if he's found her yet.'

'How am I ever going to sail,' said Liz to Steve, 'unless I manage to get away? They'll stop me. They won't let me.'

'Oh nonsense honey. If you really want to you'll sail. How can they stop you? You're sixteen. Almost a woman. Soon you'll be able to do exactly as you please. You'll be able to row the Atlantic single handed in a bathtub if you so choose. Not that I'd recommend it.' She smiled a watery smile.

'Mind you,' he continued, 'I suggest you improve your maths a bit. Danny's right there. You'll never make a navigator if you don't.'

'You're heartless. You don't care, do you?'

'I'm just being realistic.'

'But there's Marie Lamont. You still don't understand.'

'Oh yes I do. I understand everything. You think in some strange way you are Marie Lamont. Reincarnation or possession. I don't know which. But that's what you believe, isn't it?'

Liz whispered so that he had to bend to catch the words. 'I think she's inside me. She isn't wholly me but somehow she's part of me. And she won't let go. She won't leave me. She'll never

138

leave me.' It was out in the open now, the words sounding strangely thin and meaningless in the sunshine.

'And you see, Marie was burnt. She died for her ambitions.'

'But it doesn't have to be like that. It doesn't have to be the same for you.' He had to make her see that the possibility for change was there. He thought he had already done it, but evidently not.

'It's always the same,' said Liz. 'People get hurt every time. I can't help it, or stop it.'

'But why? Why must people get hurt? Why must it be the same? Tell me that.'

'She put an ill cast on her cousin Thomas Green, fisherman of this parish. Whereby it was proven that she was a witch. He was drowned. On her own admission she consorted with the devil so she deserved to die, didn't she?'

'Do you really think that she was a witch?'

'I don't know. No.'

'Or that this man was really the devil? Was really any more than some bad guy who knew when he was on to a good thing?'

'No. Of course I don't think he was the devil. Oh but she couldn't change things, could she? If she really had been a witch, maybe she would have managed to change things. She tried and look what happened to her. They burnt her. I'm so frightened Steve. I'm frightened to stay here. What will happen to me if I stay? What will they do to me?'

'What are you afraid of them doing to you?'

'Changing me. Making me conform, to their ways, to their expectations of me. I'd rather burn.'

'Yes. Yes, I can see that. But it needn't happen. You've already changed things now, haven't you?'

For the first time he saw uncertainty in her. She wavered. 'Can't you see it?' he persisted.

'No. No, I can't.'

'Come here.'

She came to him. He put his hands on her shoulders and looked down into her eyes. He saw torment and trust there. Thank God she still trusted him.

'Tom didn't drown. You saved him.'

'No. You saved him. You're the hero. You're my talisman. What will I do without you?'

'Liz. . . . Lizzie. You're confusing what you feel for me, or maybe even what you think you feel for me, with your own

139

capabilities. You don't need me. You're strong. You can do anything you want.'

'If I can do anything I want, I want to come with you,' she said. 'I want it more than anything in the world.'

It was his turn to feel uncertain. For a moment, all the years of his carefully accumulated independence wavered. Desire for her filled his mind, like the aftermath of a dream, colouring everything with its own peculiar radiance. He reached out and touched her cheek, tenderly, like a lover.

'Take me with you,' she said. 'Please take me with you. I'll love you. I'll do anything you want. Please!'

Her uncharacteristic humility shocked him. 'Shsh. Don't say that Lizzie. Don't.' What have I done to her to make her behave like this, he thought. Aloud, he said, 'How can I take you with me? You don't even know me Lizzie. You only met me a week ago and you know nothing of me. You want to rely on me but I'm not very reliable. Oh Lizzie, women do it all the time. They like to have a man to rely on, instead of taking responsibility for themselves, the tragedies as well as the triumphs. Even Marie — she claimed to be the devil's servant. Was he her talisman then?'

'Yes. Maybe.'

'He was her lover Lizzie and maybe she thought she could count on him, but she was wrong.'

'Can I not trust you then?'

'Yes, of course you can. But don't count on me to live your life for you. Listen to me. Why did Marie need to go to sea with Tom? Why not go alone?'

'She wasn't strong enough.'

'Jesus Lizzie, if she was strong enough to carry a man on her back and strong enough to bear children she was strong enough to take a boat out. OK, so men keep telling women how weak they are. How they mustn't do this and that, because they're not strong enough. And maybe you're right. Maybe Marie had to believe in it because of when and where she was born. But you — Lizzie — are you still so reliant on the opinions of men like Tom and Danny that you believe them when they tell you you can't sail! Look — you don't have to hate them for God's sake. You don't have to try to drown them either. All you need to do is say, "To hell with you all. Of course I can. I *can* do it." '

He saw something really change then, some opening of her expression.

'Love me if you like Lizzie,' he continued. 'Love me as your friend and as your equal. Rely on me to support you and help you. But for God's sake don't rely on me to direct your life. Don't exchange one form of slavery for another. Don't make me or any man into a talisman for you. We're not that important.' He took her hands. He had to make her see. 'I couldn't have saved Tom without you Lizzie. You raised the alarm. You saw him in the water. You took the boat back in. *You*!'

'I suppose so.'

'Lizzie if you really want to sail, nobody and nothing on this earth can stop you. Not now or ever. You've been afraid until now. Afraid to take charge of your life. But you're luckier than Marie. You can. So why not fulfil her ambition as well as your own and she'll leave you in peace? So will everyone else, I promise you. You've got a gift. Maybe it comes from her or maybe it's all your own. I don't know. It hardly matters. But for heaven's sake make the most of it. Don't ever give up on it.'

He lifted the little silver pendant from round his neck. It was an intricate spiral design like a maze. She had noticed before that he always wore it. 'Here,' he said, slipping it over her head. 'Take this. I want you to wear it for me.'

'What is it?'

'It's a Hopi Indian symbol. Very old. Time out of mind. As old as your stone, if not older. It stands for the feminine principle. The Mother, if you like. I thought it might bring me some luck out on the ocean, but I want you to have it now. I think you need it more than I do.'

'Won't you miss it?'

'No. I can think of you wearing it.'

Not as much as I'm going to miss you, he thought.

'But don't rely on it,' he said. 'Don't count on anything or anybody too much. Rely on you, yourself, Elizabeth Finlay. That's who you can always trust. She'll always be on your side.'

She was standing very still now, looking up at him, fingering the pendant. 'There are other fears too,' she said. 'What about those?'

'What fears?'

'Oh. You know.'

'Yes. I think I do.'

He bent and kissed her on the forehead but she stayed close, waiting, so he kissed her again, very gently on the lips. She had been kissed before by Tom and by boys at parties and had not liked it much, but this was neither awkward nor threatening. She

141

trusted him completely.

'You mean you're a little afraid of this too, aren't you?' he asked.

'Yes I am. It's all so new.'

'Oh but I can't make love to you Lizzie.'

'Why not?'

'Because it can hurt. I don't mean physically. Not if your first lover's gentle and unselfish.'

'And you would be, wouldn't you?'

'Yes. But however you look at it, it's one living being intruding on another's private space. And that can disturb the whole of you, if you don't watch out.'

He stood quietly with his arms around her, the top of her head just touching his chin. They fitted comfortably together. 'Way back in the sixties when I was at college we used to pretend it meant nothing. But it's not true. It doesn't work that way. Don't let anyone ever fool you. It'll change you. You'll never be quite the same after.'

He kissed her a third time, to wind up the charm and she responded to him. She had not known that her own body was capable of such exquisite subtlety. Then she burrowed in close to him, reaching up instinctively and stroking the back of his head where his hair grew soft and fine, sniffing at the sweet clean scent of him, like a small animal.

He let her stay there for a while because she felt so right, but then he roused himself. Her family would be missing her. They had no more time.

'There now,' he said, holding her at arms length. 'Look what you've made me do. I've broken my own resolution. I didn't want you to know.'

'To know?'

'How I felt.'

'And do you. . .?'

'Shsh.' He shook his head sadly. 'Don't say any more. Let's leave it. Mm? I'm going to take you home to your mother now.' He moved away from her with an effort and started the engine.

'One last time Elizabeth,' he told her. She came to take the wheel. He stood behind her and covered her hands with his own. Together they took the boat in.

Alice and Rose were down on the pontoon, gazing anxiously out to sea. 'Look,' said Rose. 'He's coming back in. He must have found her. I told you so.'

'You've got a welcoming committee,' said Steve. 'They knew where to find you, didn't they?' He waved at the two women and they waved back. He docked the boat just long enough for Liz to step ashore carrying her holdall. At the mouth of the marina, Liz had gone below to get the bag from the cabin where she had left it. Unzipping it quickly she had placed the precious piece of scrimshaw on Steve's pillow.

As soon as Liz was safely ashore Steve turned and went out again. Alice embraced her daughter. 'I thought you'd gone for good.' There were tears in her eyes. 'And I don't know what Danny will make of all this.'

'Does he need to know?' asked Liz, lightly.

'No. I don't suppose he does.'

'Oh mum I'm sorry if you were worried I don't know what came over me.'

I wouldn't marry Danny, not if he were a millionaire with seven yachts, she thought. But he was her mother's choice and he could be worse. She would only have to put up with him for a little while. Keep him sweet for two years perhaps and then she'd be off. University maybe. Sailing certainly. A vista of possibilities opened up before her. In spite of everything, Danny, unemployment, the state of the nation, at least the possibilities were there. Infinite possibilities. Never give up on your dreams, she thought.

'And now?' said Alice anxiously.

'I'm fine now,' replied Liz. 'Let's hurry. I want to watch the boat leave. From up on the hill. Come on.'

'On you go, you two' said Alice tactfully. 'I'll go straight back to the flat. Put the kettle on. You must be hungry.'

Aboard the *Marie Lamont* Steve gave a last wave and then headed for the open sea. He felt empty and tired as though he had undergone some immense physical exertion. He closed his eyes momentarily and saw Liz's bright young face, tasted the salt on her lips. He shivered at the vision. The boat seemed very empty without her. 'Oh hell,' he said to himself. 'Hell and damnation.'

A great wave of misery and desolation towered over him, threatening to swamp the small unstable craft of his life. He felt more alone than ever before. Always, on his voyages he had been aware of the boat, like a physical presence, like another person. Now the image of Lizzie intruded, came between himself and that intensely personal relationship with his craft.

Resolutely he focused his mind back on the boat. His *Marie*

Lamont. Gradually as he drew away from the land, the quiet presence beneath his hands and feet reasserted itself, reassured him. He relaxed, riding out the storm of emotion. Time. He needed time. Well he would find plenty of that where he was going. He turned and headed for open water.

Liz and Rose stood up beside the Kempock Stone watching the *Marie Lamont* head out towards the sun. The light just caught the white of her sails so that the distant boat was like a small silver coin, moving over the golden surface of the water. Liz touched the little silver charm at her throat. She thought of Steve alone, and content in his solitude and wished him all the luck in the world.

'Poor old Granny Kempock' she said. 'I'm glad I never pushed her in.'

'Maybe you won't need her quite so much now,' said Rose.

'Maybe I won't.'

Rose moved to stand a little apart from her granddaughter.

'You seem different.' She looked shrewdly at her.

'Do I?'

'Yes you do. Has anything happened?'

'Not today specially. No. Well. I sorted a few things out. Steve helped me. He helped me to — get things in perspective. I've had a bad time gran. That's all. It isn't over yet, but it's going to get better. I'm going to make it better. I can do it you know. I can sail.'

'I think you can.'

Rose turned to walk up the hill. 'Shall we go home now? I could do with that tea.'

'Yes. I'm coming.' Liz had one last look into the bay. The *Marie Lamont* was no more than a distant glimmer on the horizon. She thought of Steve. She could imagine him finding the whalebone carving. She wondered how he would react. She could see his face. She could still taste his mouth on hers. She could feel the long warmth of his body. But she couldn't recollect him whole. He was a beloved shadow at the back of her mind. She was young and strong and rich in promise. As she stared out to sea there was something a little hard and tempered, a little relentless in her, an awareness that had not been there before. Perhaps it was no bad thing.

'Me, myself,' she said to nobody in particular. 'I reckon it's all up to me, now.'

MARIE 1662

Marie's trial took place on March 4th 1662. She was found guilty, condemned and burned. She was sixteen years old.

Before her execution she confessed of her own free will, and asked for forgiveness.

'This is my voluntary confession without any manner of torture. I have been guilty of most terrible witchcraft. I loved my cousin Thomas and would not have harmed him, though he would not take me to sea. I now repent me of all my wickedness and may God have mercy on me. May he take pity on me and permit my atonement for all my sins, at a time of his choosing, that my soul may not burn also, but may fly free as a bird upon the waters for all eternity. Amen.'

A FLUTE IN MAYFERRY STREET

Eileen Dunlop   ISBN 0 86267 183 3

Edinburgh's new Town is the city's beautiful late eighteenth-century quarter, and a tall quiet but somewhat sad house in one of its shabbier streets is the setting for this second novel by Eileen Dunlop. Here live three members of the once prosperous Ramsay family, and when we first meet them, none of them is very content with daily life. Mrs Ramsay wonders how she can make ends meet. Marion feels her existence appallingly restricted by ill-health, and Colin pines for something he can never, he thinks, have — a flute of his own.

Award winning author, Eileen Dunlop was born at Alloa, and educated in Alloa and Edinburgh. She has worked with children all her life and is currently Head of the Preparatory School of Dollar Academy. Her novels which have won high acclaim include *Robinsheugh (Swallow)*, *Fox Farm*, *The Maze Stone*, *Clementina*, and *The House on the Hill*.

THE WAR ORPHAN

Rachel Anderson   ISBN 0 86267 185 X

What do boys think about war — especially those who
are involved with pacifism and CND? Into Simon's
well ordered and happy life comes Ha the war orphan
from Vietnam. The effects for Ha, Simon and his
family are dramatic. This beautifully written,
evocative story is both moving and intensely funny as
these two boys from different cultures on opposite
sides of the world learn to live as brothers.

Rachel Anderson has written several books for
adults and children, among which *Moffatt's Road*
(1978) and *The Poacher's Son* (1982) were both short-
listed for The Guardian Children's Fiction Awards.

NO HERO FOR THE KAISER

Rudolf Frank   ISBN 0 86267 200 7

The world closed in on Jan Kubitzky on September 1914 — his fourteenth birthday. Russian soldiers, armed with guns and cannon were in the fields and similarly armed German soldiers were in the wood. Between them lay the small Polish hamlet of Kopchovka, which had been Jan's home until the day when everything in it was destroyed. When the firing stopped, only he and Flox, Vladimir the shepherd's dog, were left alive.

'*NO HERO FOR THE KAISER* is a work so remarkable that you have to wonder why it has taken so long to reach us here. The German-born author served in the 1914 war, and wrote the book from that experience. It was banned and publicly burned by Hitler in 1933. Its acclaim, we learn continues . . . Graphic, memorable . . . it's clear to see why this book was put to the flames.'

Naomi Lewis *The Observer* 1986

THE SENTINELS

Peter Carter   ISBN 0 86267 195 7

When John Spencer's parents die his uncle packs John
off into the Royal Navy as a 'Gentleman Volunteer'.
His ship, HMS Sentinel is bound for the worst service
in the Navy, the West African Squadron, the anti-
slavery patrol.

Torn by civil war and shattered by the impact of fire-
power, the tribal organisation of West Africa is
breaking down. One man taken as a slave is Lyapo, a
farmer, captured by Dahomey warriors. Chained,
desperate, separated from his wife and children,
Lyapo is passed from trader to trader until he is bought
by the ruthless American, Kimber, master of the slave-
ship Phantom. Bound for the plantations of America,
Lyapo now faces the hazards of the high seas where,
when Sentinel and Phantom meet, he finds himself
joining John Spencer in a desperate struggle for
survival.

Winner of The Guardian Children's Fiction Award
1981.